The First String Tackling Dummy

The Player Who Never Gave Up

by

Ted Kozak

This is a work of fiction, and the places, persons, events, and organizations depicted in this novel are creatures of the author's mind. Any resemblance to any person, living or deceased, is entirely coincidental. However, it must be kept in mind that the author is highly familiar with the City of Los Angeles and its institutions so that it almost impossible to write about such a city without some reference to them.

Published 2021 by Midnight Star Press
Print Edition ISBN: 978-1-7339231-5-6

Acknowledgments

Special thanks to Jim Kerr, and Vincent Kozak who made suggestions for improvement of the manuscript that led to this book.

A special thanks to Dr. Richard Kozak who suggested the title of this book.

All errors in the manuscript, unfortunately, are mine alone.

Other Books by Ted Kozak

Chapter One

Ryan should have known that something was wrong when he heard his mother calling his name from up in the stands. He wouldn't have heard her over the crowd noise if he hadn't been behind the team bench trying to shake off an ankle sprain he received at the beginning of the second half of the game when his foot gave way while trying to elude a tackler.

His mother was easy to spot in the stands, one of the few black faces in a crowd of Hispanics and white people. She had a frantic look on her face and was pointing at someone or something at the bottom of the stands.

Ryan didn't understand what she wanted him to see. The four-foot chain link fence on the other side of the track behind the bench was lined with spectators, and he couldn't see where she was pointing.

What he didn't know was that she had been pointing at Ryan's sworn enemy, Thurman Adams, a seventeen-year-old, rail-thin punk with the crazed eyes of an unhappy rattlesnake. If Ryan had seen Thurman standing along the fence line at that moment, it would have taken his mind away from the game and would have raised an alarm as to what this thug, who had the athletic ability of a one-legged ostrich, was doing at a football game.

But there was nothing Ryan could have done about it if he had known Thurman Adams was there. It wasn't illegal to watch a football game.

A cheer suddenly went up from the stands on Saint Ignatius' side of the field. Ryan walked back to the sideline to see what was going on. His team had recovered the football at their forty-eight-yard line.

He looked at the scoreboard and groaned. His team, the Saint Ignatius Warriors, was down by four points, and there were less than two minutes left in the game. They were playing for the City

Championship against the Jefferson Heights Red Raiders, a team from an affluent suburb on the eastern side of Los Angeles County.

The game had gone well until Ryan had sprained his ankle. Jefferson Heights had come roaring back in the second half, the score 42 to 38 now in Jefferson Heights' favor. Without Ryan at halfback, Saint Ignatius couldn't match them point for point.

Ryan trotted over to his coach, Eddie Lindsey, a wise-looking Black man with a gray mustache who was conferring with Father Mike McKay, the school's principal. Ryan was hesitant to bother the coach, but Father Mike saw him and let the coach know someone was standing behind him by a quick shift of his eyes.

Lindsey turned and saw Ryan. "You're supposed to be sitting on the bench, Moore."

Ryan noticed that Lindsey was not wearing his gray fedora. It was a bad sign. The only time he took his hat off was when Saint Ignatius was losing, something that did not happen that often.

"I'm ready to go back in," Ryan told the coach.

Lindsey looked down at Ryan's left foot. The shoe and ankle had been taped up.

"Can you run with that thing?"

"The pain has gone away."

"I asked you a question."

"I think I can run."

"Pardon me!"

"I *can* run."

A cheer went up from the other side of the field. Lindsey turned to see what was happening. Greg Jones, the Warrior's quarterback, was tackled after scrambling for a two-yard gain.

Lindsey turned to Ryan. "I need you to go in and tell Jones to run T-Quick."

"That's a pass play," Ryan said. He was disappointed by the call. He was being sent in as a decoy.

"I know that," Lindsey said. "Do it."

Ryan jogged onto the field. His left ankle felt as if it had an anchor around it, but there was no pain. He didn't know it, but Coach Lindsey was carefully watching him run to the huddle.

The reaction from Jones was explosive when Ryan told him the play. T-Quick was a quick pass on a slant to the tight end.

"Dammit! What in hell is the coach thinking?" Jones asked. "We should be throwing downfield."

Ernie Salazar, the left tackle, responded. "He's thinking I can't keep that son of a bitch covering me out of the backfield."

Jones shook his head. "Ryan, can you run with that damn thing on your foot?"

"If you change the play, Greg, you won't be the quarterback next year."

Jones looked up at the sky. "Alright then. T-Quick on set."

The play didn't go well. The nose guard, a bruiser named Jeremy Trotter, burst over Ronny Patterson, the center, and threw Jones for a loss of two yards.

When Jones got off the ground, the only thing that kept him from having a few words with Patterson was the pain in his ribs.

Thankfully, the referee blew the whistle.

Coach Lindsey had called a timeout.

Ryan looked up at the stands, searching for his mother. He couldn't find her. She was no longer in the stands. He looked for the cheerleaders. He saw Denise, his girlfriend, among them.

The cheerleaders were striking a silly pose, one hand with a pom pom held high, the other resting on the hip. Ryan wondered whatever possessed Denise, a young lady with a high degree of intelligence, to join a group that pranced around like a flock of pigeons ducking a rainfall.

Coach Lindsey entered the huddle, gray fedora in hand, and got down on a knee in the mud. "First of all, there is no cussing in my huddle. You got that, Jones? I could hear you all the way from the sideline."

"But I . . ."

"You're the captain, Jones. You're responsible for this team."

"Yes, sir. No cussing."

"Second of all, I want all of you to look over at their bench at their forty-five-yard line. Do you see their quarterback and running back standing there?"

The team in the huddle looked at the opposing bench. Running back Red Meyers and quarterback Tyler Jefferson were standing on the Jefferson Heights sideline, their helmets off, hair matted with sweat, anxiously watching.

"They're afraid they're going to lose," Lindsey said. He put his fedora back on his head and looked at the scoreboard. There was seven seconds left in the game. "We're not going to lose."

Coach Nick Ferrentini, whose coaching style emulated that of a Marine Corps drill instructor, was in the Jefferson Heights huddle.

Defensive captain and middle linebacker, Buster Hollister, was exhausted, his hands on his knees.

Ferrentini scowled at him. "Damn it Hollister, straighten up and look at me. What did I just say?"

"Sir?" Hollister's voice was hoarse.

Ferrentini looked expectantly at Hollister. "What did I just say? Are you listening?"

Hollister nodded. "You want us to set wide to cover a pass or a sweep by Moore."

"That's exactly what I want. Boys, if we stop them here, we've got this game won. Do you understand?"

The team responded in unison. "Yes, sir!"

Ferrentini left the field.

Coach Lindsey was having a final word with his team. "We are *going* to win this game. What we're gonna do is run that ball right up their gut. We're going to double cover that nose guard from the right guard and blast a hole big enough to let a freight train through." He turned to Ryan. "Moore, this is your play. Take what you can get. The only guy that might cause you a problem is that middle linebacker. If Cameron doesn't block him out, can you rattle his bones?"

"Yes, sir!"

"One more play, men," Lindsey said confidently. "Make it one to remember."

"What's the play, coach?" Jones asked.

"I just told you. Double team the nose guard and handoff to Moore and improvise." He looked around the huddle one last time. "Okay team, what's up?"

The team responded with a clap. "Never give up!"

Jefferson Heights trotted to the line of scrimmage with a look of homicidal determination in their eyes; their uniforms and muscular forearms glistening with mud.

The two teams glared at each other across the line of scrimmage.

Ryan took his position behind Greg Jones, his entire concentration of the play he was about to run.

Jones stooped down over the center. He called a triple cadence, trying to lure Jefferson Heights offsides.

"Set! . . . Hut! . . . Hut!"

It didn't work. No one on defense moved.

Jones took the snap. The center and the right guard plowed into the huge nose guard, driving him to the left.

Ryan took the hand-off and charged through the gap.

Hollister, the middle linebacker, moved forward for the tackle. Cameron Parker, the slanting tight end, hit Hollister hard but bounced off him. Before Hollister could recover, Ryan drove into him like a freight train and flattened him, saying, "Bye, bye!" as he rushed past him.

Ryan raced downfield. He cut right, dodged the free safety, and crossed the goal line for a touchdown.

The horn blared, ending the game. The Saint Ignatius crowd was delirious with joy as Ryan circled out of the end zone. He stopped

dead in his tracks when he saw Thurman Adams standing behind the chain link fence alongside his two buddies.

They locked eyes with each other for a moment. Then, Thurman with a menacing smile on his face opened his Army fatigue jacket and displayed a gun tucked in his pants.

All of the sights and sounds of the Saint Ignatius victory stopped for Ryan as he stared at the gun. His teammates, delirious with joy and oblivious to the danger, surrounded Ryan and dragged him to the center of the field. He was met by the entire team who was warwhooping in celebration. They had removed their helmets, all of them proudly displaying Mohawk haircuts.

Ryan broke free from his teammates and looked for his mother in the stands. He saw her. She was smiling and wiping tears from her eyes.

At the fence, Thurman followed Ryan's gaze and saw Nora Moore in the stands. He nodded to his buddies and they left the stadium.

Chapter Two

Three months earlier

Nearly everyone didn't want Ryan to box. His coach, Eddie Lindsey, didn't. Father Michael McKay didn't. And his mother didn't, which was a surprise because she had supported her husband Kai Moore when he was a regular on the boxing card at Olympic Auditorium.

But there was this homicide detective that the family knew who ran a youth boxing program just south of the downtown business district near the Olympic Auditorium. Detective Sergeant Sid Conners knew the family because he was the one who, seven years ago, came to their house to tell Nora Moore that her husband had been shot while trying to prevent a gang of thugs from dragging a thirteen-year-old girl into an alley.

Conners felt sorry for the family and tried to help them. When Nora's husband died, she had been earning a little money by babysitting. What she earned was not enough to pay the mortgage on the house and feed her and Ryan. Conners helped her get a job in downtown Police Headquarters as a Police Service Representative.

When Ryan finished eighth grade, Conners approached Father Michael McKay and managed to get Ryan a tuition-free spot at Saint Ignatius High School. By then, Ryan was six feet tall and had the build of an athlete. He was spotted one day on Saint Ignatius' sprawling campus by Coach Eddie Lindsey who encouraged him to try out for the football team.

During spring training, Ryan ran the hundred-yard dash at a blistering pace, outperforming everyone on the team. Lindsey put Ryan on a weightlifting program during the summer of that year.

When school began in the fall, Ryan was the starting running back. In his first year, he scored an average of three touchdowns per game.

When Conners had seen what Coach Lindsey had done with the boy, he began trying to recruit the boy into his boxing program. It took him nearly a half year to convince Ryan's mother to allow him to join the program. Lindsey also objected and threatened to kick Ryan off the football team if he took up boxing. When Conners persisted and Ryan seemed interested, Lindsey relented with the provision that Ryan wouldn't box during the football season.

Ryan trained in downtown Los Angeles in a gym called Mickie's Fight Club that was located in a small, deserted warehouse near Olympic Auditorium. When Conners thought Ryan was ready, he began setting up matches for him, no more than three rounds long and always wearing protective headgear. Ryan had a talent for boxing, and Conners began thinking he had a potential Golden Gloves State Champion on his hands.

One month before Ryan's junior year at Saint Ignatius began and two weeks before the start of football practice, Conners was approached by a coach named Red Miller who wanted to set up a match with one of his fighters.

The fighter was named Thurman Adams.

Conners knew who this boy was and had watched him work out. Thurman was not an athlete. He was tall and gangly and didn't have the physique of a fighter unless he put on fifty pounds of muscle.

Conners declined the offer, but Miller persisted, saying that he was trying to get the boy away from the gangs, and he needed to keep him involved in the boxing program.

What Miller did not tell Conners was that Thurman Adams was not only a gang member but was already trying to set one up with himself as the leader.

Finally, Conners agreed to a sparring match but only after conferring with Ryan who was willing to go three rounds just to break the tedium of working out on the weights and the bags.

On the day of the match, there was a problem at the start because Thurman Adams began arguing with his coach about the necessity of wearing protective headgear. His coach won that argument. Thurman put on the headgear.

Ryan turned to Conners. "Has this guy been in a ring before?"

"It doesn't look like it, does it?"

"He has long arms," Ryan observed. "And he's tall. How do I approach him?"

"Get inside and stay there. He's got no meat on his ribs. You know what to do."

The fight was brief. Thurman came out of his corner like a mad man, flailing his arms like a duck shaking water off its feathers. He managed to land several glancing blows on Ryan's shoulders, but he also left himself wide open.

The first thought that came to Ryan's mind was that this dude was crazy. He had no discipline, . . . and he didn't know how to fight.

Ryan bided his time, backing away from the flurry of punches. A minute into the first round, Ryan decided he needed to do something to stop this nonsense. He went low under Thurman's flailing arms and landed a hard blow to his kidney. When Thurman backed away in pain, Ryan landed an uppercut to his jaw followed by a left hook.

Thurman staggered backward and fell to the floor, his head bouncing on the mat.

Ryan stood over him for a few seconds.

Thurman looked like he was finished. His eyeballs were dancing around in their sockets.

"It's over," Conners said as Ryan turned to go back to his corner.

Afterward, Ryan remembered those words for a long, long, long time. It was by no means over.

As Ryan walked backed to his corner, someone yelled, "Watch out!"

Ryan turned.

Thurman was striding across the small ring, his eyes glazed with rage, his arms spread wide, and his shoulder hunched down like a Sumo wrestler. Thurman for some reason had taken off his protective headgear and thrown it across the ring, which turned out to be a big mistake.

He was, Ryan later thought, an easy target. Ryan assumed a fighter's stance, waited for a fraction of a second, took a step forward, and threw a right hook, a left jab, and then a right hook directly into Thurman's face.

Thurman fell to the floor, blood spurting out of his broken nose. He was out cold.

It was over now. But not for the long term. For Thurman Adams, it was never going to be over.

Chapter Three

Ryan heard a voice calling him. He turned and saw his girlfriend Denise in a scanty cheerleader's uniform running toward him. Although she was just five-feet tall and more than a foot shorter than Ryan, she managed to jump up onto him. He fell to the ground with Denise on top.

He looked up at her. "What are you doing?"

"You did it. You did it!" she happily screamed.

Ryan looked up into her face and couldn't help thinking that this was the most intimate contact he ever had with his girlfriend. He smiled, but the smile faded away when he heard his teammates laughing at him.

"Man, that girl hit you harder than anybody else tonight. She should try out for the team." The speaker was Ernie Salazar, the left tackle.

Denise got off the ground, laughing. Ryan got to his feet and hugged her. She reciprocated but leaned forward like she always did, not allowing Ryan to get too close to her body. Ryan resisted the urge to grab her by the butt and pull her into a bear hug. He realized that doing something like that might end their relationship. He would have to live with the memory of Denise sitting on top of him, her bottom in contact with his chest.

The two of them, holding hands, watched a couple of Saint Ignatius players with Mohawk haircuts doing a whooping war dance.

"It's going to be a hot time at Dinsie's tonight," Ryan said.

"Oh no," Denise said. "Why not do something normal, like go home and have hot chocolate and watch some television."

Ryan smiled. "See you later. At Dinsie's"

Denise bit her lip. "I'll be there."

Dinsie's was a small walk-up hamburger stand, an island in the middle of a vast parking lot surrounded by an ancient business district just south of downtown Los Angeles. The parking lot behind Dinsie's was the scene of a rite performed every Friday night after Saint Ignatius won a football game.

"I just can't believe you boys. You win the championship, and you act like a bunch of fools," Denise told Ryan as they got off the bed of a pickup truck that had just arrived at the parking lot behind Dinsie's.

"You just don't understand football, Denise," Ryan said. "If we don't do the dance, the tribal gods don't let us win."

She stopped and stared at him in disbelief. "You better not let your momma hear that. She'd do a tribal dance all over your body."

The massive parking lot was full of cars parked in a huge circle. There was a heavily attended beer keg in the back of a pick-up. Hundreds of spectators, all of them Saint Ignatius students, some standing, others seated on car hoods, all of them solemnly watched their team engage in a tribal rite that was evocative of Stravinsky's Rite of Spring.

It was what the Saint Ignatius football team did after every victory, which was nearly every Friday night in the fall. Coach Lindsey knew about it, and so did Father Mike. They let the celebration go on for an hour before they and the rest of the coaches swooped down and scattered the players.

It was a game played after every game. Let the players have their fun but break it up before anyone got seriously drunk or hurt.

The team was formed into a huge football huddle with the players hunched down, each player with his arms around the shoulders of the players next to him, moving slowly in a circle while a band nerd in the back of a pickup truck slowly beat a bass marching drum. The players took exaggerated giant steps, circling to the right, raising their feet in the air slowly, then slapping their feet to the ground in rhythm with the booming drum.

BOOM–SLAP–BOOM–SLAP–BOOM–SLAP!

The rite always lasted five minutes. It was followed by a series of cheers led by the yell leader and more celebrating as some of the players tried to score with the cheerleaders while others spent more time getting refills at the beer keg.

But the celebration didn't usually go long into the night. The participants knew from previous experience that it would come to an end at precisely sixty minutes after it began. At the appointed time, Coach Lindsey and Father Mike and their minions would ride in like the Valkyries from Norse mythology and put an end to the celebration.

Ryan and Denise made their escape from the revelry and caught the night bus to Echo Park where they both lived. They got off the bus by the lake and began walking up Laguna Avenue, a slight slope into a residential area consisting of one-story bungalows that were built before World War I.

Two chattering boys on skateboards raced downhill on the sidewalk toward them. Ryan was walking with his arm on Denise's shoulder when he saw them. He shouted a warning and began to pull Denise off the sidewalk to avoid a collision, but the boys jumped the greenbelt and landed on the street.

As they raced by, one of the boys yelled, "Shots!"

Ryan and Denise turned and watched them race downhill. The boys turned right onto Echo Park Avenue without slowing down.

"What did they say?" Denise asked.

"I think they said 'shots'," Ryan said.

Suddenly, Ryan stopped and stared straight ahead.

"What's wrong?" Denise asked.

"Stay here!"

Ryan began running. He turned the corner onto the next street where he and his mother lived. When he got to the sidewalk in front of the house, his worst fears were realized. The heavy metal screen door and the front door were ajar.

He took a deep breath, then ran up to the porch and stopped at the door. The wood around the strike plate on the door frame had been ripped apart. He hesitated, sensing that someone was in the house even though he saw nothing moving.

At first, it was quiet, but then he heard a loud commotion coming from the back of the house. It sounded as if someone was throwing things around.

Ryan entered the dimly lit front room. Crucifixes and religious artifacts decorated the walls. A photo in an ornate picture frame on an end table showed Ryan's father, wearing boxing gloves and shorts, in a fighter's pose.

He carefully looked around the room for anything that was out of place but at the same time trying to remember where his father kept his gun. He looked to the left and saw a chair lying on its side next to the open entrance to the dining room.

A human form was lying on the floor next to the dining room table. He crossed the room slowly, his eyes fixed on the body. When he got there, he found that the body was his mother. She had a bullet hole in her face just above the nose, and a pool of blood flowed around her head.

Ryan gasped for air. He dropped to his knees in anguish, his arms outstretched. Later, he could not remember how long he had been on his knees when he heard a loud crash coming from the back of the house and then the soft murmuring of voices.

It could have been seconds; it could have been minutes, but the effect of the crashing noise electrified him. It was like the ringing of a bell signaling that a fight was about to start. Whoever had killed his mother was still in the house.

He got up and unconsciously wiped something sticky from his pants. He moved quickly to the front room and then to the hallway leading to the bedrooms at the back of the house. Light spilled out from his mother's bedroom at the far end of the hallway.

The crashing noises continued.

Ryan moved slowly and quietly down the hall until he reached the door to his mother's bedroom.

He looked inside.

From the doorway, Ryan saw Thurman Adams pulling drawers from a dresser and dumping the contents on the bed. His cousin, Calvin Slater, was bent over the bed, rummaging through pieces of costume jewelry. Calvin's younger brother, Billy, was on the far side of the room and in the process of retrieving a gold-colored ring from a jewelry box on a cosmetics table.

Ryan knew the Slater brothers. When he was ten, he hung out with Calvin and Billy at the skateboard park not far from where Ryan and his mother lived. He hadn't seen much of them since they dropped out of school and left the neighborhood.

Billy examined the ring he found in the jewelry box. "It's a fight ring. Must have been the old man's."

Thurman dumped the contents of another drawer on the bed. "That ain't shit. I got two of them already and they ain't worth crap."

"When did'ya ever score a fight ring? You never won no fight."

"I ain't never said I won 'em, dawg-shit."

Billy walked towards the doorway, his eyes fixed on the ring in his hand. He sensed someone standing in front of him and he looked up.

Ryan's thunderous right hook slammed into his astonished face. The blow drove him backward, and he flipped over the back of Calvin who was still bent over the bed. Billy bounced off the bed and fell to the floor.

Calvin straightened up and said, "Hey! Why did you do that?" He heard a grunt and turned. He saw Thurman, his mouth open, staring at the doorway. Calvin turned toward the doorway and saw Ryan. He drew a .45 semi-automatic pistol from his waistband.

Ryan lunged forward and tackled Calvin before he could bring the gun up. They fell to the floor and struggled for possession of the gun. It went off, discharging into the wall. Ryan rolled off Calvin and tried to force the gun loose by twisting his arm backward.

Thurman, panicked, ran for the hallway, but then stopped and turned. He fired a wild shot at Ryan. The bullet went past Ryan, missing his nose by inches, and hit Calvin in the shoulder.

Calvin's gun fell free as he grabbed his shoulder and wailed in pain.

Ryan grabbed the gun.

Billy, dazed and bleeding from the mouth, got up on his knees. He fired two wild shots at Ryan.

Ryan raised the .45 automatic pistol he had taken from Calvin and returned fire at Billy, hitting him in the chest and knocking him to the ground with the force of a Mack truck.

Using the edge of the door as cover, Thurman fired another wild shot at Ryan.

Ryan spun around and fired back. The bullet hit the doorframe, and a splinter of wood hit Thurman below the right eye. He howled like a wounded puppy and disappeared.

Hearing a groan behind him, Ryan turned to see Calvin, cradling his bloody shoulder and trying to get up.

Ryan, in a rage, aimed the gun and fired two shots at point-blank range into Calvin's chest.

Thurman Adams, blood streaming down his face from the cut below his eye, ran down the hallway. He tripped and fell on a carpet. When he got up, he had lost his bearings. He shook his head, realizing he needed to steady himself. Behind him, he heard two gunshots, and he began running again.

Thurman dashed outside onto the front porch into a blaze of flashing emergency lights as several police cars, their sirens screaming, roared into position in front of the house. He stopped suddenly on the sidewalk, dropped his gun, and threw up his hands.

Ryan, gun in hand, ran out of the house and stopped on the porch when he saw the police.

A police officer using a loudspeaker said, "You on the porch, drop that gun *now!*"

Ryan dropped the gun. What he heard next didn't make any sense.

Thurman was pleading with the police officers. "Shoot him! Shoot him! He killed my cousins."

Later, Ryan was on the porch of his mother's house, listening to Sergeant Sid Conners. The detective sergeant, an ex-boxer in his forties, was wearing a brown hat with a stingy brim, a white short-sleeved shirt, a clip-on black tie, and sharply creased black trousers, He was only five foot four, and if it weren't for the 9mm. Beretta FS semi-automatic in a shoulder holster, he would have looked more like a used car salesman than an experienced homicide detective.

Conner's voice was muted, drowned out by the bustle of police activity.

"Listen, Ryan. What you just told me about what happened in there was off the record. I can't take an official statement from you without a relative or guardian present. Do you have any aunts or uncles who live in town?"

"I don't have any aunts or uncles that I know of. My father was an orphan."

"What about your mother?"

"She came from Nebraska. She talked about a sister who lived there but she died. I don't think there is anyone else in our family . . . except me."

"Well, there's also Eddie Lindsey."

"The coach?"

"Yep."

"He's not my relative."

"But he's an attorney. He can help you."

"He's not an attorney. He's a teacher."

"Lindsey was an attorney before he became a teacher. I'll call him. I'm sure he would be glad to help you out with the interview."

Ryan looked out onto the street. Denise was talking to another detective on the sidewalk. A black van with the words marked CORONER in white drifted down the street and parked near the front of the house.

Tears streamed down from Ryan's eyes. His attention was momentarily diverted by someone screaming.

Thurman Adamas sat handcuffed in the backseat of the police car parked at the curb. His face, contorted in venomous rage, pressed against the closed window.

Ryan could hear what he was saying.

"Let me outta here. I'm gonna kill you, punk! I will track you down and kill you! I will kill you like a dawg! Do you hear me punk? Lemme go! Lemme outta here!"

Three hours, later, a red-headed man with a pock-marked face and stocky build entered the interview room at Police Headquarters and sat down in a chair across the table from Ryan Moore and Eddie Lindsey. He introduced himself as the Officer-in-Charge of the Metro Gang Unit and said he had a few questions to ask Ryan.

Lindsey objected at once, saying that Ryan had already been interviewed in depth by Sergeant Conners and his partner, and he wouldn't permit another interrogation.

"I've been briefed by Conners, Coach Lindsey. All I'm interested in is what information Ryan has about the gang that Thurman Adams runs with."

"He already told that to Conners."

"But he personally knew Thurman Adams," the man paused for a few seconds, looking through a folder he had placed on the table. He found what he wanted and then looked up at Ryan. "These two kids, Calvin and Billy Slater. Before tonight, when did you last see them?"

"Not since they dropped out of school," Ryan said. "A couple of years ago."

"And you ran with them?"

"I never ran with them," Ryan said, misinterpreting what the man meant. "We had skateboards."

"Have you ever been a member of a gang?"

Lindsey shot up from his seat. When he spoke, there was anger in his voice.

"Where in hell are you going with this? We don't even know who you are. You haven't told us your name. Get Conners back in here."

The man, unperturbed, looked at Lindsey and said, "My name is Freed, Coach Lindsey. All I really want to know is where did the kid learn how to shoot a gun?"

"Damn you! Get the hell out of here!"

Ryan laid a hand on Lindsey's arm. "I can answer that question, Coach. If you let me."

Lindsey looked at Ryan. He nodded and slowly sat down, his eyes locked with Freed's.

"My dad taught me, Mr. Freed," Ryan continued. "He took me out to the desert a couple of months before he died and taught me how to shoot."

"Okay. And where is the gun now?"

"I think Sergeant Conners has it."

Freed's eyebrows raised. "Conners has it?"

"Yes, sir. It was the gun Calvin Slater had. I shot him with it."

Chapter Four

Saint Ignatius High School sat on twelve acres on a hill overlooking downtown Los Angeles. Behind the school was a newly constructed gymnasium, a state-of-the-art football field with real grass, a football practice field with a running track around it, and a baseball field, all provided by a graduate of Saint Ignatius who was in the NBA.

The school was an architectural hybrid of castle and prison, its bleak entrance flanked by grey, stony, crenelated towers. The campus was surrounded by a seven-foot masonry wall. One portion of the north wall next to the football practice field was different. It was made of fading red brick and was somewhat higher than the wall that surrounded the rest of the campus. This wall not only shared a boundary with the high school but also enclosed the gardens of a three-story brick mansion called the Ignatius Center.

The building, which was formerly a convent, was now the home of four priests, one of whom was Father Mike McKay, the principal of Saint Ignatius High.

It was morning and students of various races and ethnic groups hustled into the school. One of them was Ryan Moore who was dropped off at the front entrance by Coach Eddie Lindsey.

Later, the bell ending the second period had rung and the central hallway was filled with noisy students on their way to third period classes. Ryan strode purposefully down the hallway toward the chemistry lab. He was escorted by two football players, both of whom were on their way to shop class. His escorts were bruising lineman, both over six-foot tall, both weighing over two hundred fifty pounds, and not the kind of people you would want to piss off.

Ryan sensed that something was about to happen when he heard a loud voice seemingly coming out of nowhere.

"Watch out!"

The chatter ceased and students scrambled out of Ryan's path to reveal a skinny kid wearing an oversized jersey and droopy basketball shorts, a blatant violation of the school's dress code. He approached Ryan and his buddies in a funny loping motion that resembled the way a kangaroo might walk if it could no longer jump.

The boy's eyes seemed as if he were staring at something a thousand yards away.

Ryan relaxed. Fortunately, Ryan's buddies never let their eyes off the stranger.

Just when Ryan thought the boy was going to pass, his eyes involuntarily twitched in Ryan's direction. He pulled out a large knife and spun around to face Ryan.

It was a big mistake.

A mistake that landed him in the hospital with a broken jaw and three broken ribs.

The two bruisers charged into the kid and drove him into the lockers with a loud crash. They stood aside, holding the kid up by his shirt to let Ryan have a go at him.

Ryan did not disappoint. He pounded fist after fist into the kid's face until he slid down onto the floor.

The next eight months seemed to Ryan as if he were in prison. At first, he lived with Coach Eddie Lindsey in his unconventional home on a hillside overlooking Silverlake Reservoir.

Ryan had never seen another place like it. The house was decorated with such an odd assortment of furniture and decorations that didn't seem to go together, but when looked at as a whole seemed a perfectly sensible way to decorate a bachelor pad.

The arrangement as a place to stay for Ryan was temporary, because Eddie Lindsey, a well-respected coach of one of the largest Catholic high schools in the City, had lots of girlfriends who liked to pop in anytime they felt like it.

Ryan found himself guessing when he woke up in the morning which one of the dozen or so women he would find at the breakfast table. He sometimes had trouble concentrating on what he was eating, since some of the women weren't overly shy about what they wore when they came down for breakfast in the morning.

Meanwhile, a County agency called Social Services tried to find Ryan a foster home in the area near the high school and that wasn't working out. There were a lot of married couples who would gladly take a sixteen-year-old boy in, particularly when the boy was a good student and an astounding athlete, but not when they found out that the boy in question had killed two gang members and had nearly beaten another to death.

Things got worse at school. One day, three gang members were stopped by security as they tried to enter the school. It was learned after questioning they had been asking students about when and where Ryan was taking classes.

And then someone in a beat-up Chevy took a pot shot at Ryan as he left school one day. The bullet would have killed a girl if she hadn't been clutching a load of books to her chest that smothered the bullet.

Ryan had to be taken out of the school and quickly before someone got hurt.

Without waiting for approval by Social Services, Father Mike pulled Ryan out of school and then convinced the agency to allow Ryan to be placed with him in the former convent adjoining Saint Ignatius High School. Ryan at last had a place to live on a more or less permanent basis, but for him, it was not a long-term solution. He could no longer go to classes at Saint Ignatius, and he could no longer see Denise. It didn't even look like he would be allowed to play football next fall.

The Ignatius Center was a nice enough place to live. Three other priests lived there besides Father Mike. One was a retired priest, a grumpy old man who had been a chaplain with the Marines in Korea and had problems walking because he had lost some of his toes to frostbite. And there were two other priests in their thirties who each had a parish of their own. One was uproariously funny, and the other was deeply introverted and quiet, which was unusual for a priest.

The food at the mansion was relatively good. Three women rotated in every day and prepared their meals on a volunteer basis. The meals were always a surprise because each of the women had her own way of making something as simple as an omelet.

More importantly, Ryan was able to continue his education while living at the Ignatius Center. His teachers volunteered to come over to the former convent on their breaks and go over their lesson plans with Ryan.

The memory of his mother and her funeral never really faded away, but as time passed, Ryan felt the pain inside him begin to go away, only to return when Sergeant Conners dropped by one morning to tell Ryan that Thurman Adams' trial was coming up and that he needed to meet with the assistant district attorney to prepare his testimony.

Ryan had already testified at Thurman's preliminary hearing and that didn't go well. When Ryan entered the courtroom, Thurman leaped up out of the chair and climbed over a table to get at Ryan, only to be forcibly restrained by courtroom deputies.

It took over an hour to get Thurman to settle down enough that the hearing could proceed. Even then, he sat in a chair alongside his defense counsel, muttering to himself and glowering at Ryan as he testified. The threat of two burly deputy sheriffs standing behind Thurman kept him from doing anything else.

As a result of the hearing, the judge, who had listened with rapt attention as Ryan described the gun battle in his mother's bedroom, found there was sufficient evidence to set the case for trial on three counts of murder, a result that Ryan didn't completely understand until Sergeant Conners explained that under the felony murder rule, Thurman was also being charged for the deaths of the two gang members that Ryan had shot.

A trial date was set but then continued to another date which caused Ryan further anguish, because each time he was reminded of the upcoming trial, the pleasant thoughts he had embraced in his mind of his mother was overwhelmed by the horror of what he had witnessed the night she was murdered.

Ryan was growing impatient with his living situation and his inability to attend school. One morning after breakfast, he stopped Father Mike as he was heading out the door.

"I need to talk to you, Father Mike. I can't stay here for the next two years."

"I know that, Ryan. I'm working on it. You have to be patient."

"I'm thinking about joining the Marines."

"You're only sixteen. They won't take you."

Ryan didn't bother to tell the priest that one of his former teammates who was eighteen had given him his birth certificate to use to get into the military.

"I look eighteen."

Father Mike took off his black fedora and said, "Let's go into the library."

The library was where Ryan spent a good part of his day studying. It was a pleasant place to study even though the smell of fresh varnish didn't have a chance of overwhelming the musty smell of old books. Even though the oak-paneled library was loaded with obscure books on religion, it had a nice section that included all the readable and nonreadable classics from Aristotle to Somerset Maugham.

Ryan was working his way through the Jules Verne novels in the evening since the only television in the Ignatius Center was monopolized by the old priest who watched Eternal Word television station during the day, and the younger priests who like to watch old reruns of Gunsmoke and Rawhide in the evening.

"Let me ask you this," Father Mike asked Ryan. "Assuming you graduate from high school, what would you prefer to do? Go into the military or go to college?"

"I'd like to play football in college."

"What about beyond that?"

"I don't know."

"Mrs. McConnell says you're the best writer in her composition class."

Ryan shrugged, not knowing where Father Mike was going with this. "I learned from my mother. She wrote short stories and some poetry. She made me read a lot and then write a summary of what I read."

"I didn't know that about your mother. Did she ever get anything published?"

"I think so. A short story or two."

"Good. The important thing right now is to get you through high school with grades good enough to get into college. Do you agree?"

"I also want to play football. I can't do that while I'm here."

"I guess I should have told you this before, but I've been working on something to help you do that. I've been talking to two high school administrators about getting you into a regular high school. One is the school founded by Father Mallory just outside of San Diego."

"You mean the one with the good football team?"

"Right. Saint Thomas Academy. I may be able to get you a scholarship. It's a boarding school. You would be able to live on campus."

Ryan immediately thought of Denise. If he went to Saint Thomas, it would be unlikely he would ever see her again. But he had the same problem here. He had been told he couldn't leave the grounds of the mansion because Thurman's friends were still looking for him. On top of that, Denise had told him that her parents had forbidden her to see or speak to him again.

"And the other school?"

"It's not so far away."

"Okay."

"Are you ready for this?"

Ryan nodded.

"It's our biggest rival. Jefferson Heights."

Chapter Five

It turned out that Father Mike's brother was the principal at Jefferson Heights, and his mother worked there as a guidance counselor. The school was located about thirty miles east of downtown Los Angeles in an upscale residential community that was surrounded by hills on three sides and enclosed by the Pomona Freeway on the north. The area to the south of the freeway leading up into the hills was upper middle class, and the area to the north of the freeway was working class, making for an interesting mix of students who attended the school.

Ryan didn't like the idea of attending Jefferson Heights High School, but he didn't like the idea of attending Saint Thomas either. When he was a freshman, his team had played them, and it struck him that the school was very militaristic. Most schools allowed their football players to stand on the sideline while watching a game.

The Saint Thomas players were required to sit on the bench during a game. Worse yet, when their coach called a player up from the bench, the player had to stand at attention while the coach talked to him. And on the football field, their players were the most intense players that Ryan had ever seen. It seemed as if the team was composed of robots.

But there were problems with Jefferson Heights also.

A lot of them.

After dinner one night, Ryan asked Father Mike if he could talk to him. They met in the garden behind the Ignatius Center.

"What's on your mind, Ryan?" Father Mike asked.

"I have a few questions about Jefferson Heights."

To Ryan's amazement, Father Mike pulled a cigar out of his jacket pocket and lit it. Ryan stopped and looked at the priest. It was the first time he had ever seen the priest smoke.

"Okay."

"They know who I am at Jefferson Heights. They know my name and they know what I look like. Word would get out that I go to school there."

"How many times did you take your helmet off during the game?"

"I dunno. A couple of times."

"What kind of haircut were you wearing?"

"A Mohawk."

"You don't have a Mohawk now and you look different. So, you let your hair grow out a little longer. They won't recognize you."

Ryan thought about it for a moment. Father Mike was right. The Mohawk had given Ryan a wild look, a look that was completely different from the way he usually looked.

"What about my name? People will know it."

"We'll change your first name. There won't be any problem arranging that. I know the principal at Jefferson Heights."

"Okay," Ryan said doubtfully. "So, who is going to drive me out there every day?"

"No one. You'll be living within walking distance of the school."

"Seriously? With who, . . . I mean with whom?"

"That'll be a surprise."

Ryan frowned. "What kind of surprise?"

"It's like a Crackerjack box. You never know what's in it until you open it."

Ryan thought he had heard something like that before, but he couldn't place where he heard it.

"So, what do you think?" Father Mike said.

"There's another problem, Father Mike. A big problem. Jefferson Heights already has a starting running back, Red . . . "

"Red Meyers."

"He's pretty good," Ryan said. "I doubt if the coach will let me have any playing time."

"Then, you'll have to beat him out, won't you?"

"He knows their system."

"So, you can learn their system."

"I dunno, Father . . ."

"I don't think we have any alternatives, but I will keep looking."

The Ignatius Center where Ryan stayed didn't have a weight or exercise room, nor was the garden large enough for jogging. Ryan felt like his body was stagnating and that he needed to do something about it. Then one night it occurred to him how he could remedy that. The high school was next to the mansion and had two separate tracks for jogging. Maybe, he could even get into the weight room if he were lucky.

Around midnight, he crept out of the mansion into the back garden. He had no problem climbing over the wall since it had a decorative finish that made it easy to gain a foothold. It was a short jog across the baseball field to the quarter-mile track that circled the football practice field.

He was on the second lap when he saw a figure standing on the track in the darkness in front of him.

Ryan stopped and sucked in a deep breath.

The dark figure had a black object in his hand that looked like a gun, and Ryan considered running back to the mansion.

A second later, a flashlight came on, temporarily blinding Ryan.

"Damn boy, you about scared me half to death," a booming voice said.

Ryan raised a hand to shield his eyes.

"What are you doing out here, Moore?" the voice asked.

Ryan relaxed when he realized the man knew his last name. "Are you the night guard?"

"Damn right, I am. What do you think you're doing out here so late at night? It's past midnight."

"I'm working out."

"Why don't you work out during the day?"

"Father Mike won't let me leave the mansion. I need to stay in shape. This is the best place to do it."

From that night on, Ryan had a place to work out. The night security guard's name was Frank Johnson, and he was a retired Air Force master sergeant. Johnson not only let Ryan use the track every night but let him into the weight room as well and arranged for the weekend security guard to do the same.

The winter/spring semester passed slowly. Easter came and went. One day, Ryan took a break from his studies by walking out into the backyard of the mansion and heard some familiar noises coming from the other side of the wall. It was the first day of Spring practice for the Saint Ignatius football team, and Ryan found it was difficult to keep from wanting to vault over the wall and joining them.

A week later, he had a big surprise when he vaulted over the wall onto the grounds of Saint Ignatius. The playing fields were lit by a full moon, but it wasn't until he got close to the football practice field when he saw it was occupied by several dozen dark figures who appeared to be in some type of organized formation.

He stopped when he saw them, trying to process just exactly what he was seeing. One of the figures emerged from the group and began walking toward him. He was wearing a football helmet. He was also carrying a football helmet and shoulder pads. He offered them to Ryan.

"We thought you'd like a little moonlight scrimmage," Greg Jones, the quarterback of the Saint Ignatius High School Warriors said.

Ryan put on the helmet and shoulder pads. He was greeted enthusiastically by his teammates when he joined the huddle. Among them were five new guys, replacements for the seniors who were about to graduate.

Jones called the play, an option to the wide side. The huddle broke and Ryan took up his position behind Greg Jones.

The nose guard, Andy Barron who had a crooked smile on his face looked at Ryan. "Hey, Moore. Just because we were teammates doesn't mean I won't rip you apart when I get hold of you."

Jones stood up from his position under center. "Damn it, Barron. We agreed this was going to be a no tackle scrimmage. No one is to get hurt."

"Got it, boss man." Barron's voice sounded anything but sincere.

On the first play, Jones pitched the ball out to Ryan on the option. He ran thirteen yards before he was touched.

They scrimmaged for an hour. At 1:32 a.m., after thanking his teammates for what they had done, Ryan, feeling exhilarated, vaulted over the wall into the backyard of the mansion.

Before he went to bed that night, Ryan realized how much he missed playing football. It was then and there that Ryan decided he was going to be playing for Jefferson Heights next fall.

Chapter Six

Just as the semester was winding down at Saint Ignatius High School, Ryan was called to the District Attorney's office to prepare for the trial of Thurman Adams which was scheduled to begin the following Monday. Sergeant Conners with two uniformed officers in a separate police car providing security escorted him to the office of the District Attorney on Temple Street in downtown Los Angeles. They waited in an outer office for fifteen minutes before the assistant district attorney, a pert young lady in her late twenties came through a security door. She had a grim look on her face.

She looked at Ryan just briefly and gave a tiny smile, her attention quickly shifting to Sergeant Conners who had taken off his stingy brim. "I'm sorry," she said, "there's not going to be a trial. Adams escaped this morning."

Conner's reaction was explosive. "How in the hell did that happen!"

Ryan was amazed at how quickly Conners recovered from his emotional outburst and sprang into action. He turned to the two officers who were with them. "415 East 23rd Place. Let's go!"

Conners ran out of the office, Ryan and the two officers following.

Ryan was barely into the car as Conners drove off, the wheels of his car screeching in protest.

"Where are we going?" Ryan asked.

Conners didn't answer. Instead, he picked up the microphone and with a sense of urgency in his voice told the dispatcher he needed two patrol units for back-up at the gas station at 20th and Los Angeles. He put down the mike and said to Ryan, "When we get there, you stay in the car and get down," leaving Ryan to wonder what in the hell was going on.

When Conners parked his car at the abandoned gas station on the corner of 20th and Los Angeles, two additional police cars were already there. On that day, Ryan learned that teamwork was not just a practice that was needed to be successful on the football field but could be applied to just about anything that involved groups of people.

He watched from the car as a half dozen police officers gathered around Conners and bent over a drawing that he had laid on the hood of a police car. The men talked for less than two minutes before they broke huddle and sprang into action.

When Ryan thought about it later, he thought that the way Sergeant Conners led the charge on the house where Thurman Adams once lived with his mother was as precisely executed as a football play. The uniformed officers got into their cars and followed Sid Conners onto East 23rd Place. They stopped a half block down a street consisting of single-story bungalows that looked like they hadn't been painted in years.

Conners turned to Ryan as he got out of the car. "Stay down and whatever happens, don't get out until I tell you to."

Ryan watched as the police officers rushed a bungalow with peeling paint and took up positions around it. Conners, holding a 9mm. Beretta in his right hand, calmly and confidently walked up the sidewalk to the front door of the house, He rapped on the door with the gun and stood aside. One of the police officers using a handrail as a brace pointed his semi-automatic Glock at the door.

A minute later, the door was opened by an overweight Black lady who looked like she was dressed for church. Ryan watched as she and Conners talked for a minute. Finally, she stepped aside, inviting Conners into her home. Two uniformed police officers followed.

It was then that Ryan noticed a can with a label on it that was on the porch near the door. It looked about the size of a soup can.

He wondered what it was. Some kind of message, maybe? He

thought about getting out of the car and telling Conners about it but decided against it. It probably wasn't important.

Five minutes later, Conners came out of the house. The police officers gathered around him, and they talked for a few minutes before Conners returned to the car. He got into the driver's seat and turned to face Ryan.

"I didn't expect to find him here, but you never know."

"That was Thurman's mother?" Ryan guessed.

"Yes. A very nice lady. Adams hasn't lived there since he was thirteen. She knows he escaped from jail but hasn't seen nor heard from him in at least two years. We'll put a stake-out on the place anyway. I believe he might be back."

"Why do you think, he'll come back?"

"He doesn't have any money. If he can't find a place to rob, he'll come here to get food." Conners looked at the house. "Do you see that can on the porch? It's a can of chili. Thurman's not welcomed back into her home, but she always sets a can of food out for him. Maybe, we'll get lucky and he'll come by to pick it up. Maybe, we'll even get luckier and someone will find a way to put rat poison in it."

Two days before the semester ended, Father Mike walked into the library where Ryan was being tutored by Miss Morganowsky, an American History teacher who had the figure of a teenage ballerina. Father Mike nodded at the teacher, who got up and left the room.

McKay sat down, a worried look on his face. "Some of Thurman Adams's former associates are out on the street looking for you."

"They've always been looking for me, Father. That's why I'm here and not in school."

"This is different, Ryan. Thurman has offered a $500 reward to anybody who can tell him where you are."

Ryan sat back in his chair and stared at the priest. "How can he do that? Where did he get the money?"

"Sergeant Conners thinks he's robbed several liquor stores."

Maybe, Ryan thought, *I should get out of here and find Thurman before he finds me.*

"What are you thinking, Ryan? You look like you want to say something."

What I should have done, Ryan thought, *was to kill the bastard when I had the chance.*

"I need to get out of here," Ryan said listlessly.

Father MacKay stood up. "I agree. How long will it take for you to gather your things?"

"Fifteen minutes for what I got here. I need to go back to the house and pick up the rest of my things."

McKay sat back down. "We got a problem," he said wearily.

Ryan stared at him. "What kind of problem?"

"Somebody set fire to your house two nights ago. It's gone."

The house had been up for sale ever since last Christmas. All traces of what had happened there had been removed by Coach Eddie Lindsey. The problem was that history had a way of being persistent. You could remove blood and gore, but you couldn't remove history. California real estate law required that a disclosure form be completed when a house was listed for sale, and the minute that a prospective buyer learned what had happened there ended whatever desire they had for buying the place.

There was insurance of course, about $250,000 worth, and the lot was valued at another $100,000, but under the terms of the trust that Ryan's mother set up, he couldn't touch that money until he reached eighteen. All he could receive until then was $500 a month for his living expenses.

By the time he packed what clothes he kept at the mansion and was in Father Mike's car on the way to Jefferson Heights, he had put the house, the money, and Thurman Adams out of his mind. He did that by imagining a massive steel wall falling down in his mind, closing off his memory, and sealing off the bad history.

The problem was Thurman Adams had no such steel wall that interfered with his memory. The only thing he thought about was finding Ryan Moore and killing him.

Chapter Seven

Ryan had never been to Jefferson Heights before, although he played against them in the City Championship game last Fall and the quarter finals a year before, so when Father Mike pulled his black Ford Taurus off the freeway, he was amazed at what he saw. The area south of the freeway was on a flat slope that was enclosed on three sides by green hills. He leaned forward and looked up through the windshield and could see that the hills were laced with winding drives.

Father Mike saw him looking and said, "The higher up you go the more expensive the home. But you won't be living there. My mother lives north of the freeway at a place we used to call the ranch."

They passed a Catholic church called Saint Aloysius, and Father Mike leaned over to look at it as he drove past. Ryan suspected the priest had been baptized and confirmed there. They then turned left on an immaculate residential street of older homes with well-kept and well-watered lawns. After a few hundred yards, they passed a large parking lot on the left with a football stadium a hundred yards behind it and then the school itself, a compound of low-slung buildings with stuccoed walls painted beige and trim painted in burgundy.

A sign out front proclaimed, JEFFERSON HEIGHTS, HOME OF THE RED RAIDERS. Another sign with changeable letters read, WELCOME BACK STUDENTS. VARSITY FOOTBALL HERE VS. FOOTHILL 8/29.

The campus was immaculate as the residential area it was set in, but it didn't have the walls and chain-link fence surrounding it that Saint Ignatius had, and there were no gang markings sprayed on the walls of the surrounding community. Other than a few cars parked in front of the office, the campus was devoid of any activity.

Father Mike pulled his car up to the curb across the street from the school.

Ryan's face was clouded with gloom as he looked over the campus. "I'm not sure this is a good idea, Father."

"They're not going to know who you are, Ryan. You're enrolled here under a different name."

Ryan had taken the first name of his father, Kai Moore, but had retained the last name. He unhappily looked over the campus. "I played football against these guys. They're going to know me."

"The only time they saw your face was through a facemask. And last year, you were wearing that ridiculous-looking Afro-Mohawk. Do you seriously think anyone on this campus would recognize you right now?" Father Mike let out a deep breath. "Look, Ryan, if Buster Hollister walked by right now, would you recognize him?"

"Who?"

"He's the middle linebacker you blew by on that last play last year."

"I dunno, Father. Linebackers look alike to me, . . . fat, dumb, and ugly."

Father Mike smiled as he restarted the engine, but he reconsidered and turned off the ignition.

"Listen Ryan, there's something you need to know about this place. I know that you think that football is your ticket to a college scholarship, but the coach here runs the team like he owns it. He plays favorites. Things are different up here in the Heights. Don't be disappointed if you don't get to play as much as you would like."

Ryan stared across the street at the school, thinking for a moment before he answered. "I know how to run a football better than Red Meyers, Father Mike."

The area north of the freeway in Jefferson Heights was littered with older houses that showed little signs of pride of ownership. While most had lawns that had been recently watered and cut, a significant number of houses had dried weeds out front.

When Kai, (Ryan had begun thinking of himself as Kai now) saw gang signs scribbled on the walls, and that some of the houses had security doors and chain link fences out in front, he was puzzled.

"Why all the gang signs here and none around the school?" Kai asked Father Mike.

"It's because of the football team, Ryan."

"It's Kai from now on, Father. What about the football team?"

Father Mike smiled. "They're the biggest gang on campus and they let everyone know it."

"You mean, they're vigilantes?"

"Not in so many words. But they let the gangs know that the area south of the freeway is off-limits."

They crossed the main thoroughfare called Walnut Boulevard, and the area changed from residential housing to industrial and manufacturing buildings. Father Mike turned the car left onto Driskell Street and passed several warehouses and small industrial shops and then a row of bungalows built in the 1920s. At the end of the cul de sac was a sprawling ranch house built in the Western style with a wraparound porch on a one-acre lot. In a vast field beyond the house was a small herd of cattle grazing near a windmill.

Father Mike pulled his car onto a gravel driveway lined with yew bushes and bordered with flowers and parked next to a first edition red Mercedes 450 SEL with its convertible top down.

The entrance to the house consisted of a heavy-duty screen door and an inner door made of heavy oak that was partially open. Seconds after Father Mike rang the doorbell, Edna McKay, a petite woman in her mid-sixties wearing an apron, emerged from the kitchen, wiping her hands on a towel. She smiled and unlocked the screen door and Father Mike gave her a big hug.

"Hello mom," Father Mike said as he sniffed the air. "Cooking again?"

"I'm baking, not cooking–baking!" Edna replied. "I'm baking for the church. The only problem is that fat old Father Murphy samples so much of the goods after Mass that we don't make enough money to make it worthwhile."

Kai, a borrowed suitcase in his hand, had not moved from the porch.

Edna McKay, a big smile on her face, waved him in. "Don't just stand there, come in!"

Kai hesitantly offered a hand to Mrs. McKay. She ignored it, grabbed him by the forearms, and looked into his face.

"Well, your nose doesn't look broken to me!"

"Huh?"

"Michael said you were a boxer, . . . like your daddy. Why no broken nose?"

"I box, Missus McKay, . . ." Kai paused, taking a glance at Father Mike. "I mean I used to box. Not many people laid a glove on my face."

"Well, no matter. Welcome home, Kai. That's your name, isn't it?"

When Kai nodded, she pulled him closer, making him feel extremely uncomfortable. Edna McKay was in her mid-sixties, but she was an attractive-looking woman, petite and trim, with lively green eyes. She was wearing jeans and a loose-fitting blouse in a colorful floral pattern.

"My name is Edna," Mrs. McKay continued. "Don't call me by that Missus thing again. It makes me feel old, and I don't like to feel old. Now come along and let me show you to your room."

As Edna led him to a hallway off to the left, Kai looked around the living room. It was large, perhaps the largest living room he had ever seen in a house and contained a mixture of Western antiques and old furniture. He would have expected an old musty smell from the age of the antiques, but the room was permeated with the pleasant odor of vanilla that probably came from the kitchen.

Several religious artifacts in the form of small paintings showed various poses of Christ walking through the barren landscape of Judea, looking as if he were searching for something. The images of Christ in a house filled with antique Western-style furniture was something Kai had never witnessed before.

The first room along the corridor was a large study. Except for the desk, computer, and printer, it looked as if it were a chapel because of the numerous religious icons and artifacts on the walls. The remaining rooms, three of them, all bedrooms, were as large as the study.

Edna McKay led Kai and Father Mike into the farthest bedroom at the end of the hall. The bed was large with a headboard made of carved dark wood. The room had an old-fashioned desk with cubbyholes that was located between two windows that looked out onto the large field behind the house. On an antique dresser was an old photograph of a football player posing as if he were a Sumo wrestler.

Kai set his suitcase down and went to take a closer look.

Edna McKay came alongside him. "That's my son, . . . Father Mike, when he was about your age."

Kai turned and saw Father Mike standing just inside the doorway.

"You played football?" Kai asked.

"I even graduated from high school."

"What position did you play?"

"Middle linebacker."

"Oops," Kai said sheepishly, remembering what he had said earlier about linebackers being fat, dumb, and ugly.

Kai found that he liked living with Edna. An agreement was made regarding rent. There was none. Kai could keep the $500 a month from the trust fund, and Mrs. McKay, or Edna as she preferred to be called, would provide him with free room and board as long as he followed her rules.

As for the rules, Kai quickly learned there were few; he was free to come and go as he please, provided he keep Edna informed of where he was, and when he planned to return. This restriction was not to control him Edna explained, but for making sure he was safe, considering the threat posed by Thurman Adams.

Kai learned that the house had been in the McKay family for over a hundred and fifty years. The property had originally consisted of several thousand acres and had been sold off parcel by parcel in the 1930s until only the house and one acre remained of what had been a cattle ranch. The cattle out in the field didn't belong to her, but they were kept far enough away from the house to keep them from being a nuisance.

Another advantage to living with Edna was that she was one of the school's guidance counselors. As a consequence, Kai was able to get his first choice of the two electives that seniors had available to them. He chose Creative Writing and Journalism.

Football practice was scheduled to begin in three weeks. School was scheduled to begin in four weeks. The first football game with Foothill High School was scheduled to begin at the end of that first week.

Kai couldn't wait, not for the school to start, but for football practice to begin.

Chapter Eight

Thurman Adams also had a busy schedule. He spent his days trying to find out how Ryan Moore had managed to disappear from the face of the earth. He spent his nights dreaming about what he was going to do when he found him.

The humiliation he experienced by the fists of Ryan Moore wasn't the only reason he wanted revenge. Moore had killed Calvin and Billy Slater, his cousins and best buds.

Life at home with his mother had been dull, which was why he ran away from home when he was thirteen. She didn't even have a television. There was nothing to do at home that interested Thurman, so he took to spending more time at the Slater house than his own. Both of their parents worked and there were a lot of things the boys could do that kept them busy. Fun things. Like watching television and sneaking girls into the house during the day. And when that wasn't enough to keep them busy, they began ripping off people's houses while they were away at work, stealing their most valuable possession just for the hell of it, and throwing what they didn't want to keep into the lake at Echo Park.

Now, his cousins were gone . . . just like that . . . and all because of Ryan Moore.

When Thurman escaped while being transported in a prison van, the first place he went was to his aunt and uncle's home. When Thurman's aunt saw who was at the door, she rushed to the phone to call the police. When Thurman realized what she was doing, he took off running down the street.

A few minutes later, a car pulled alongside him, and just for a moment, Thurman thought it was the police. But it wasn't. It was his Uncle Jack Slater who told him to get into the car.

Thurman's uncle was a security guard at the massive City Produce Market located just south of Olympic. He drove Thurman to an abandoned warehouse next to the produce market and gave Thurman a key, telling him that he could find a cot in one of the front offices. He also warned him not to go out during the day. Before he left, he told Thurman to leave the girl alone, that she belonged to him. Thurman had no idea what the hell he was talking about.

One day later, the uncle returned. He gave Thurman a revolver with a four-inch barrel and some money. He warned him not to rob anybody working in the Produce Market, and that if he needed something to eat, he should go to Joe Leone's stall in the market who would give him some fruit. He warned Thurman again to leave the girl alone. Before Thurman could ask, "What girl?", his uncle was gone.

Thurman quickly found out what he was talking about. A mentally deficient teenage runaway named Lucy lived in the same warehouse. The first time that Thurman saw her she was shooting a rat with a pellet gun. Thurman watched her as she picked up the rat by the tail and cryptically said, "Mice one", and then dropped it in a plastic bucket she was carrying.

Lucy lived in an office at the opposite end of the building. She was an attractive girl, even though she did little to make herself look halfway decent, and Thurman suspected his uncle was visiting her on occasion.

Thurman listened to what his uncle had said and stayed away from her. His bed was an Army cot in a small office, his blanket a throw rug; his pillow a rolled-up olive green parka that he stole and frequently wore at night while he wandered the streets trying to find out where Ryan Moore was hiding.

He lived on a diet of canned food, chili being his favorite, beef stew his second most favorite. His diet also included some fruit provided by Joe Leone. Occasionally, Thurman would eat breakfast at a small rundown diner called Dodgers on the outskirts of the City Produce Market that was frequented in the early morning by working-class black men after finishing their shift at the market that fed most of Southern California.

Thurman carried the small revolver his uncle gave him tucked in his belt behind his back, and when he needed money, he held up a liquor or convenience store. He evaded being easily identified by changing his appearance when he robbed a store. Whenever he felt the need to replenish his money, he wore what he believed was the perfect disguise; a Navy knit cap and looser fitting clothes that made him look heavier than he really was.

And he had an uncanny sense of hearing. He could recognize the sound of the roaring motor of a police car as it raced in response to a robbery call versus the sound of just about any other car speeding on the street.

Having never learned how to drive, Thurman either walked or took a bus to wherever he was going. He knew that his appearance was such that he would draw the attention of the police who were looking for him. So, he came upon the idea that if he had a girl with him when he ventured out on the streets and the police saw them together, they would ignore him.

He found that even though Lucy ignored his presence and very rarely spoke to him, she was agreeable to going out with him at night as his escort. They would take the side streets to wherever he was going, and he would hold her by the hand, making it look like they were boyfriend/girlfriend out for a stroll. She would willingly go along because Thurman provided her with food, money, and ammo for her pellet gun.

His only recreational activity was playing pool, which he did in a rundown bar on East Fifth Street that never bothered to check i.d.

Lucy refused to go inside the bar. She would sit outside on a milk crate, watching for the beat cops while Thurman played pool and drank beer inside. Whenever she was bothered by someone, she would run them off by displaying her pellet gun which looked like a Colt .45 pistol.

Thurman maintained the pretense of having a gang of his own, but it was only for the purpose of having eyes and ears on the street listening for any sign of Ryan Moore. By and large, gang members were afraid of Thurman, having heard wild rumors about how he strangled a police officer when he made his escape, which was untrue. Thurman had simply walked out the back door of the prison van that had been left unlocked by the guard.

Any doubts that anyone in the gangs had about doing what Thurman wanted was quashed when they saw the wild look that burned in his eyes at the mere mention of Ryan Moore's name. Thurman thought about killing Ryan Moore nearly every minute of the day. He dreamed at night about killing Ryan Moore. He could actually picture in his dreams shooting and killing the boy who killed his cousins.

But he had a nightmare one night that made him realize what a lousy shot he was. He dreamt he was in the bedroom where his cousins had been killed, and Ryan Moore was pointing a gun the size of a rocket launcher at him.

Thurman couldn't remember how many shots he had fired in his dream at Ryan that night, but they were all misses. Maybe, it was the revolver he carried with its lousy four-inch barrel. Maybe, he would have to get a different gun, one that was more accurate. Maybe he even needed to spend some time practicing with it.

But there was one thing he knew for sure. There were no maybes about it. He was going to find and kill Ryan Moore.

Chapter Nine

One week before school started, Edna McKay dropped Kai off in the parking lot next to the Jefferson Heights High School gymnasium. He got out of the car and looked around. A group of boys, all of them tall, most of them sleekly muscled, were walking into the gymnasium.

"Are you going to be all right?" Edna McKay was looking at him, concerned.

"I'll be all right," Kai said, as he removed his gym bag from the back seat of her car. He waved at her and began walking apprehensively toward the gym when a black Mercedes sedan driven by a woman cut him off by pulling alongside a row of parking spaces.

The woman behind the wheel hadn't even noticed that she nearly ran over someone. Kai tried not to look irritated as he threw a glance at her as he walked around the back of the car.

She was a blonde in her late thirties, maybe early forties, and dressed like a teenager, wearing a hot pink tennis outfit that clashed with the formality of the Mercedes. She reminded Kai of an aging Barbie doll.

As Kai rounded the back of the sedan, he saw a tall kid that he recognized from last Fall getting out of the car. It was Tyler Jefferson, the Jefferson Heights quarterback. He said, "Goodbye Mom", to the woman in the car, slammed the car door shut, and hurried toward the gym carrying a large duffle bag.

Kai followed him, and as he did so, he sensed that Tyler's mother had craned her head to look at him as he passed. He ignored her and headed straight for the gym, passing an empty parking space with a painted sign containing a single word printed on it. It read, COACH. The word, DUH, was printed above it with a black marker pen.

Kai entered the noisy gymnasium. It was filled with about ninety wannabe players, most of them lined up behind a table occupied by one of the coaches and three girls who were assisting the boys with filling out paperwork. Others who had finished the paperwork were being shepherded into the bleachers by another coach who demonstrated the fact that some people in this world should never wear shorts. He had knobby knees, and his shorts failed to cover them.

The first person that Kai encountered when he entered the gym was a petite girl with a sparkling face. She had sandy brown hair with blonde highlights, and it took Kai a moment to realize that the reason why her face sparkled was that her make-up had glitter in it.

She handed Kai a leaflet, and said, "Hey studly! I'm Amy. Read this over, and if you still think you want to be a big-time football player, go over to that table and sign up with Coach Prince."

Kai looked at the leaflet. It was entitled *Coach Ferrentini's Rules*. The entire page was repetitiously covered with the same words, NO DRUGS, NO BOOZE.

He looked down at Amy after he finished reading it. "So, it's my understanding that the coach has no problem with unbridled sex?"

Amy smiled. "Bridled or unbridled. There is no way he could ever hope to stamp out something as popular as that on this campus."

Kai stared at her for a moment thinking about the implications of what she said and then returned her smile. "Thank you, Amy. Nice to meet you."

As he approached the end of the line, Kai experienced a moment of panic when some of the players turned and stared at him for just a moment too long before they turn away. It was then he realized he might be the only Black trying out for football. Later, he would find he was the only Black in the entire school except for three teachers and several cafeteria workers.

Kai got into line behind a tall boy. A look of surprise crossed the boy's face when he saw Kai, but the smile returned just as quickly. He offered his hand. "Hi. I'm Angelo Rodriguez. You're new here."

"I am new here," Kai replied. "My name is Kai."

"Kai?"

"Kai Moore."

"What position do you play?" Angelo seemed blessed with a perpetual smile on his face.

"Running back. A little at the corner, but mostly offense. How about you?"

"First string tackling dummy."

Kai, bewildered, cocked his head. "What did you say?"

Angelo smiled broadly at his reaction. "First string tackling dummy. I will be quarterbacking the scout team offense. They need fresh meat for Hollister during practice so that he doesn't kill one of our starters."

"Do you play much? In the game, I mean."

"Next year's my year. Unfortunately for you, we already have a starter at running back. What are you, junior, senior? Where have you played before?"

Kai had not figured on having to come up with a fake background to match his fake name.

"Up north."

"Where up north?"

Before Kai could come up with an answer, Angelo broke off the conversation and looked toward the door. A monster of a boy with a baby face stood next to Amy, looking over the leaflet she handed him with a disgusted look on his face.

"That's our center, Oliver Brown," Angelo whispered. "We've been waiting for him to show up. They won't let him forget what happened last year. Watch what happens when someone spots him."

A moment later, one of the boys in the bleachers spotted Oliver Brown as he was talking to Amy. He rose to his feet and using cupped hands as a megaphone, yelled out across the gym in a booming voice. "What's the color of shit?"

There was a resounding long drawn out response by nearly everyone in the gym. "Brooooown!"

Brown threw down the leaflet and stared indignantly around the gymnasium.

Angelo turned back to Kai. "Redstone pulled that stunt in a game last year. It drew Brown offsides right when we didn't need a penalty, plus it cracked everybody up . . . except for the officials and the coaches. Those guys are born serious."

A moment later, Brown joined the line behind Kai. He looked at Kai with his head cocked and begged for sympathy. "If your name was Brown, would you want to be called 'shit'?"

Kai sympathetically shook his head 'no.'

"Ollie, everyone I know says you ain't shit," Angelo said.

Oliver Brown didn't get the insult.

When Kai got to the table where players were being checked in, he handed his paperwork to the assistant coach, Wally Prince, who looked it over, then looked up at Kai with a smile and handed him a schedule for the week.

"Welcome to Jefferson Heights, Moore. Take a seat in the bleachers."

The day went longer than Kai expected. Once everybody was checked in, the players were ordered by Coach Prince to form a herd, which meant that everybody had to bunch up in the bleachers in front of him.

Coach Nick Ferrentini, who was a legend in high school football circles and who had reportedly turned down offers to coach at the college level, strode into the gymnasium from a side door and stood in front of the players a full minute before speaking. He waited until the boys had quit whispering to each other before he began talking.

His first announcement had to do with the restructuring of high school football in Los Angeles County. There were now twelve teams in the Mission League, and the League was divided into a western division and an eastern division. Jefferson Heights was in the eastern division. After the regular season, the winners of the two divisions would play for the League Championship.

"That means before we even get to play for the City Championship," Ferrentini said, "we have to beat the winner of the western division."

He paused for a moment to let the murmuring die down. "Can anybody here tell me who is now in the western division?"

There was silence in the gymnasium.

"Well, I'll tell you who it is. It's Saint Ignatius . . . the same goddamn team that whipped us in the City Championship last year."

Kai shifted in his seat. For a moment, he thought the Coach had glanced in his direction when he mentioned Saint Ignatius.

"That means, we have a tough season ahead of us if we want to be in contention for the City Championship," Ferrentini continued, "and that means you *will* follow my rules to the letter."

The Coach spent the rest of his time on his rules. At the top of the list was abstinence. That meant no booze and no drugs, but he didn't leave it at that. He went on to talk about not getting involved in indiscriminate sexual relations. That comment caused some mumbling among the players about what exactly he meant. All of them understood what sexual relations meant, but the word 'indiscriminate' was not one that most of them heard when it was used to describe sexual relations.

"When you leave here for the field house," Ferrentini continued, "you will be given a Rules Manual by the girls. I expect you to read it tonight. You will find there are severe penalties for certain indiscretions, like forgetting to put away your equipment in the locker, like leaving candy wrappers on the floor, like coming into *my* field house with dirty cleats. No cleats are to be worn in that building. We have a state-of-the-art field house that is spotless, and I want it kept that way. You will be responsible for what's in the Manual beginning tomorrow."

He paused for a moment.

"I have also been advised by Mr. McKay that there will be a requirement that players have to maintain a C or better average to play football on this here team. I don't want to have to explain, like I did last year, that taunting another player is not the same as trying to teach him something. I don't want dimwits on my team. If you have problems with any of your classes, we will have tutors available for any of you that need them. Any questions?"

He looked over the players with what Kai thought was a wild look, defying anybody to speak up.

"No? No questions? Then I take it that everybody understands what I said. Coach Prince, the floor is yours."

Wally Prince, the assistant coach, talked about the schedule during the coming week. There would be two hours of conditioning drills in the morning beginning at 7:00 a.m. and two hours of practice beginning at 5:00 p.m. He strongly advised the players that they should not eat any solid food before the conditioning drills in the morning because they didn't want the practice fields fertilized by foreign substances. Anybody who regurgitated their breakfast on Coach Ferrentini's practice field would be required to work with the facilities maintenance team for a total of five hours.

Kai followed the boys out the back of the gymnasium to a large brick building called the Joseph and Anna Meyers Field House. It was obvious to Kai that the building couldn't have been more than a year old. It had offices for the coaches, separate locker rooms for the varsity and junior varsity teams, an office for the medical staff, a room for the trainers with spas and ice baths, and a massive work-out facility that was as impressive as the one at Saint Ignatius High School.

It took more than an hour of waiting in line for Kai to check out his practice equipment. He nearly forgot about the rule about not wearing cleats in the locker room until Angelo Rodriguez reminded him. He put his cleats on just outside the Joseph and Anna Meyers Field House where there was a long bench designed for that purpose. It wasn't until later that he learned there was a connection with the name on the field house and a player on the team.

Chapter Ten

Nearly two hours after Kai had entered the Jefferson Heights gymnasium to sign in, he stood in line with the prospective backs and receivers next to an offensive coordinator named Simpson. The players hoping to make the team were waiting to be timed for the forty-yard sprint.

Kai just happened to be in line directly behind Red Meyers. He studied the boy who was about to become his adversary. Red was two inches taller than him but had none of his muscular development. He had a shock of flaming red hair with trimmed sidewalls that made him look like a cartoon of a woodpecker.

When Red turned and saw Kai standing behind him, he was momentarily taken back, but then came on strong. "Who the hell are you?"

Kai blinked at the dripping arrogance in Red's voice. "My name is Kai Moore. Who the hell are you?"

"Everybody knows me. What planet did you come from?"

"I'm sorry, I should've known who you were. What threw me was I thought you were one of the water boys."

Red glared at Kai, clenching his fists, his florid face turning scarlet, his freckles turning darker.

Kai returned the big staredown, ready to block any blow that Meyers might be thinking of throwing.

No problem if I have to take on this asshole, Kai thought. *He acts tough but he looks soft.*

He then realized that if he had to fight this boy, it would be he who would be thrown off the team. This was Red's home turf and he already had a starting position on the team.

There was a thaw in the tension when Coach Simpson had to yell to get Red's attention. "Meyers, you're up! Get your butt up on the line!"

Red turned away from Kai and took a set position on the forty-yard line, one hand on the ground, his body canted forward.

Kai resisted the urge to kick him in the butt.

Coach Wally Prince was forty yards away at the goal line, his left hand raised high and a stopwatch in his right hand. Next to him were Coach Nick Ferrentini and Joe Meyers, a redheaded executive type.

When Ferrentini yelled, "Go," Prince dropped his hand. Red launched out of the three-point stance and sprinted downfield toward the goal line.

Prince clicked the stopwatch as Red ran past. He looked at it, frowned, and then showed it to Ferrentini.

Joe Meyers butted in and looked at the watch. He groaned.

Ferrentini looked up at Red. "You're slower than last year, Meyers! What the hell you been doin' this summer?"

"I've been working out," Red muttered defiantly.

"Doing pushups on cheerleaders is not what I'd call working out."

"Nick, we've had a rough summer," Joe Meyers said, "but he has been working out. Give him another chance tomorrow."

Ferrentini nodded but said nothing.

Just as Coach Prince was about to signal Kai to begin his run, the principal of Jefferson Heights High School, Franklin McKay, joined the group, and Ferrentini immediately turned his attention away from Red Meyers and toward him.

"Mr. McKay, do you know Joe Meyers? Joe, this is our new principal, Franklin McKay."

Franklin McKay smiled and offered his hand to Meyers. "I know you and your wife have been great friends to the school, Mr. Meyers. Is your son still on the team?"

"Of course, he is," Joe Meyers said indignantly, pointing at Red.

"Red Meyers is our running back," Ferrentini said. "We expect him to set the State rushing record this year, though he's not near as fast as he was last year."

"I see," Franklin McKay said, as he studied Joe Meyers' face. "I apologize for my lack of knowledge of your son's athletic achievements, Mr. Meyers. I haven't been caught up to speed yet on anything except administrative paperwork."

Joe Meyers nodded stiffly. "You related to that priest that runs Saint Ignatius?"

Franklin McKay nodded. "He's my brother."

"Nick, hate to interrupt," Prince butted in, "but we got the new kid on the line."

"Send him off," Ferrentini said.

All four men watch as Kai took a three-point stance on the forty-yard line.

Prince raised and immediately dropped his hand. Kai launched himself out of the three-point stance like a rocket and crossed the goal line seconds later. Prince clicked the stopwatch and stared at it, looked at Ferrentini, and then looked at the stopwatch again.

"Well?" Ferrentini said, sensing he had just witnessed something unusual.

Prince showed the stopwatch to Ferrentini. "Nick, I think it's close to the State record for the forty and he did it on the turf!"

"My Lord," Ferrentini said. "Where in hell did he come from?"

Franklin McKay looked away, a smile on his face.

Ferrentini glanced at a worried Joe Meyers and then turned and smiled at Coach Prince. "He'll be a lot of help on your scout team, Wally. He should be able to give the defense a major tune-up."

The timed trials were followed by thirty minutes of intense calisthenics, and then a long run up into the hills of Jefferson Heights. The team followed one of the trainers who was riding a Vespa.

Kai found that the run up into the Heights was instructive about what money could do for you. He always had an interest in cars, and he noticed how they were able to predict the layers of wealth in Jefferson

Heights. At the base of the hill around the high school, Fords, Chevys, and Toyotas predominated. Higher up, the Lexis, Infinitis, Cadillacs, and other stylish sedans became evident until there was a gradual shift to Porsche and Jaguar sedans and a few Ferraris.

A half hour later, Kai Moore was the first of his team to enter a cul de sac on a bluff that overlooked the high school. Kai had wisely allowed Red Meyers and several other boys to take the lead early in the run because he didn't want another confrontation with Red. But after five minutes, they had slowed down at a pace that was unacceptable to Kai, so he took the lead.

There were three girls with nicely tanned and sculptured legs wearing red jerseys and white shorts waiting for them with water bottles and sport drinks at the end of the cul de sac. Kai drank his bottle of water at the edge of the bluff while looking down on the flat area below the hills. The football stadium was the first open space below him. Even though he had run over two miles to get up here, the stadium below looked as if it were only three football fields away.

"You can head back down now. Morning practice is over," the trainer said.

Kai nodded and started downhill.

Later that afternoon, Ferrentini and Prince were called to Principal McKay's office and were informed that Kai Moore was the Saint Ignatius running back who had helped defeat Jefferson Heights in the City Championship game last year.

Ferrentini's first reaction was that he couldn't stop laughing at the irony of it. When Franklin McKay told him the reason why Kai was enrolled under an assumed name, Ferrentini stopped laughing.

"What about security?" Coach Prince said. "Isn't it dangerous having him here?"

"We have security on campus. We have off-duty police officers at games. But none of that is as important as keeping his real identity a secret."

"If that's true, why tell us?" Ferrentini asked.

"Because when you see what this boy can do at practice, you are going to start asking questions about where he came from. I am counting on you to make sure we head off any problems."

"We haven't talked about this before, Mr. McKay," Ferrentini said, looking worried. "I'm assuming I have full authority to run my program as I see fit."

"You do."

"I already have a good running back, and that is not going to change."

"I understand. That is your prerogative."

"Now back to this boy. I think you would agree with me that the best thing for him is to keep a low profile."

"I agree. What do you have in mind?"

"We'll keep him on the scout team. Barring any unforeseen circumstances, he won't get any playing time and won't attract any attention in the press."

Chapter Eleven

Kai found out he had been assigned to the scout team later that night. The bad part of it was that he would not be able to take any hand-offs or catch any passes from Tyler Jefferson, and it would minimize his opportunity to play in a game. The good part was that Angelo Rodriguez was the quarterback of the scout team and loved what he was doing. His infectious smile had a positive influence on everyone around him.

After dinner that night, Kai went out to the patio behind the house and looked over the Rules Manual. The first three pages dealt with motivation and encouragement for the players to strive for their best in practice and to be aggressive in games. The remainder listed the rules that the players were expected to follow and the punishment for each violation. There were many of them, the least severe punishment was twenty push-ups for throwing trash on the floor. If a gum or candy wrapper was found on the floor next to a locker, it was assumed that the player who had that locker dropped it. It occurred to Kai that this rule could be easily abused by a player who wanted to cause problems for another player.

Most of the punishments for a rules violation involved spending time working with the facilities maintenance crew. And several violations such as drug use, theft, fighting, an arrest by the police, or getting a girl pregnant would get you kicked off the football team.

That night Kai had a crazy thought about setting Red up, so that he could get caught in a violation that would get him kicked off the team. By the next morning, Kai realized how stupid and wasteful that kind of thinking was. The only proper way he should beat Red for a starting position on the team would be to show the coaches how much better he was at running the football than Red.

But the chances of doing that while on the scout team were minimal.

The playbook that each member of the varsity team received on the following day was a lot more complicated than the Rules Manual. The scheme at Saint Ignatius was based on a diagram for either a running or passing play that was given a name and number (or numbers). Each schematic had its own offensive set-up, the designated runner in a running play, the primary and secondary receivers if it was a passing play. and the routes each should take.

Since there was little correlation between the name of the play and how it was to be run, the players on offense were required to commit the plays to memory. Kai noted that the playbook at Jefferson Heights was virtually the same as the one at Saint Ignatius with the exception that the names and numbers were different.

Following the early morning workout, the entire team reported to a theater-like classroom next door to the field house. Coach Prince stood on a podium next to a green chalkboard with the names of twenty-five plays written on it.

"We play Foothill, next week," Coach Prince said. "These are the plays we'll be using in that game. You are expected to memorize the first ten plays and know how to execute them by tonight's practice. We will add five plays a day until you have learned them all."

There was a collective groan from the players designated to play offense as they walked out of the classroom.

Memorizing the plays was the easy part for Kai, but he realized that executing the plays might prove to be more difficult for him. Since he was on the scout team, he would have little opportunity to run any of the plays with the starting offense.

Evening practice began with calisthenics for a half hour followed by drills. The team had three quarterbacks for passing drills, so Kai got a lot of practice running the routes they were going to use against Foothill, and he had no problem catching the bullet-like passes from Angelo Rodriguez.

After an hour, the team split into two practice groups, the first string offense led by Tyler Jefferson against the scout defense, and the first string defense against the scout offense led by Angelo Rodriquez.

Foothill had not been on the Jefferson Heights schedule last year, and the coaches couldn't get Foothill's game film until the end of the week, so the scout team used Jefferson Height's offensive plays against the starting defense.

Kai got to run the ball several times, breaking out of the route that the play called for when he found the line clogged. He also caught all three of the bullets that Angelo threw at him. Overall, he had an impressive practice.

But Coach Casey, the defensive coordinator, was not impressed by what he had done. He was not watching what the players on the scout team were doing. He was primarily concerned with the performance of the starting players on defense and spent all his time screaming and yelling at them for their numerous mistakes.

Chapter Twelve

When Kai arrived at the high school with Edna McKay on the first day of school, he was amazed at what he saw. During the week before school started, it was quiet on campus and even serene. Now, it bustled with activity. The street in front of the school was clogged with expensive SUVs dropping off teenagers under the watchful eyes of maroon-blazered, security officers.

Edna parked her Mercedes 450 SEL in the teacher's lot behind the administration building and looked at Kai before getting out of the car.

"You know where your homeroom is?"

"I do."

"And you know where my office is?"

Kai nodded.

"If you have any problems . . ."

Kai held up his hand. He thought he knew what Edna might be trying to tell him. He was only the third Black ever to be enrolled in the high school.

"I didn't have any problems with the team," Kai said. "I don't think I'll have any problems on campus."

Kai found he was largely ignored by other students as he walked in the hallway toward his homeroom. Everybody seemed too busy renewing old acquaintances to notice him. The first thing he noticed was the way the girls dressed, which was quite different from Saint Ignatius where there was a dress code.

Nearly every one of the girls wore shorts or miniskirts showing off their tanned and shaved legs, including the chubby girls who had sausage-like calves. There wasn't one particular style that predominated among the boys, some dressed sloppily as all hell, others dressed like they were going to church. He noticed that at least a half dozen Hispanic boys wore black T-shirts and khaki trousers. Kai, who was sensitive to gangs and their paraphernalia, wondered if this was a sign of gang membership.

It was in his first class that morning, Journalism, that Kai encountered the school's most unconventional character. The classroom was full and most of the desks were taken, so he headed down a row toward the back of the room where there were still empty seats.

The classroom was noisy. The teacher, Marcus Robinson, one of the three Black teachers in the school according to Edna McKay, was busy at his desk doing paperwork.

Two girls near the back of the classroom noticed Kai as he walked down the aisle. They whispered across the aisle to each other and snickered. One of them wore a mini-skirt so short that Kai could see she was wearing circus-like, polka dot underwear. He took a seat behind the girl with the colorful underwear and noticed that the students across the aisle on either side of him were also girls.

It smelled like he was in a perfume factory.

He no sooner than sat down when a slender hand with overly long, polished fingernails reached across the aisle and gently touched his forearm.

"You must play football," the owner of the hand said.

Kai turned to find the hand belonged to a girl with long wavy auburn hair and wearing scanty clothing. She was extraordinarily pretty even though she had a perpetually puzzled expression on her face that hinted she might have been born with a brain a few clicks off center.

"I can smell a jock from a mile away," the girl suddenly said.

The girls in front of Kai began laughing.

"I really didn't mean it that way," the girl said in an offended tone of voice to the girls who were laughing.

She turned back to Kai. "I used to be a cheerleader, so I can tell if someone's a jock."

"Used to be a cheerleader?" Kai said.

"Well, yes. I flashed the North Hills team last year just as they were coming out of a time out."

To Kai's amazement, the girl pantomimed lifting up her blouse.

The girls in front of Kai broke down hysterically with laughter, nearly falling out of their seats.

The girl with auburn hair turned her attention back to the girls in front of her. "It helped our team," she said earnestly. "It really did, and don't say it didn't!"

She turned back to Kai.

"North Hills should've had a touchdown. They kept looking to see if I'd do it again. They fumbled and we got the ball back. And I got kicked off the squad for doing that! Can you believe it?"

Kai stared at the girl in disbelief.

On his way out of the classroom, Marcus Robinson motioned Kai to join him at the desk. He stood up as Kai approached.

"A word of warning, Mr. Moore. You play football, don't you? So, you know the coach's rules. You need to be careful with that Robbins girl. She's the reason why the coach put in that rule about not getting a girl pregnant."

"Do you mean the girl sitting across from me?"

"Who?" Marcus paused for a moment. "Oh no. I'm talking about the girl with blonde highlights in front of you. Her name is Sally Robbins. If she tells you there's something she'd like to show you in back of the field house, don't bite. She's trouble."

"Who was the girl sitting next to me?"

"The one talking to you?"

"Yes."

Marcus Robinson smiled. "That's Patty Jefferson, daughter of one of the richest men in the Heights. She's quite a show-off, but she's also quite harmless."

The team met an hour earlier than usual on the first day of school in the classroom next to the field house. Coach Ferrentini turned down the lights and showed an entire game film between Foothill and Redstone. He stopped the video on several occasions to demonstrate how Foothill played what they called their 'Power Offense'. It involved putting their biggest players in the backfield and then running option plays that tried to wear the defense down by blasting through them.

Kai quickly saw that Foothill had several sets of backs that they rotated after every play. He also saw that Foothill was content to get four to five yards to a run and that the fifth or sixth play, depending on the circumstances, was almost always a pass.

The video was followed by a brief announcement by Coach Prince that the coaches over the weekend had made diagrams of twenty plays that Foothill always ran, and that following calisthenics and warm-up, the first string defense would scrimmage against the scout team using those plays.

After calisthenics, the scout team and the starting defense formed up on a field adjoining the main practice field. Coach Prince knelt in the center of the scout team huddle with a clipboard that showed a diagram of a play.

"Okay people, we play Foothill Friday night, so we're gonna run some of their plays. This is the first play Coach Casey wants us to run." He held up the clipboard showing it to each of the players in turn. "Does everyone know what he's going to do? This is pretty much like our Two Dive Right. Angelo Rodriguez under center, Jerry Morris at half, Kai Moore at tail. The play is a dive between the right guard and right tackle, Rodriguez hands off to Moore who dives through the two slot. Does everybody have it?"

The team nodded.

"Right guard and right tackle, do you see your blocks?"

They both nodded.

"Okay, Angelo, it's all yours."

The defensive unit was still huddled up with Coach Casey when the scout team offense broke out of their huddle.

They had to wait for nearly a minute before the starting defense broke the huddle and took up their positions.

Buster Hollister, the middle linebacker, pointed at Angelo and raised his other arm defiantly. "Hey, Angelo! Your ass is grass and I'm a power lawnmower! I'm going to buzz right through your line and chop your ass into taco meat."

Kai looked back at Coach Prince who stood there smiling. Coach Lindsey at Saint Ignatius would have never allowed anything like that to happen on a practice field. Something as simple as that could lead to a fight. He began to wonder if there wasn't something about swearing or using words with a racist meaning in the Rules Manual. He couldn't remember.

But then Meloni, the scout team right guard and biggest player on the line, raised his hand, and said to Hollister, "If you want Angelo, you'll have to come through me, you fat turd!"

Hollister's first reaction was to spin in a circle like an angry dog. He then ran up to the line, pushed aside the nose guard, and pointed at the football.

"Meloni, you see that football? That's your dumb ass!" Hollister lifted one foot in the air and flattened the football with a loud bang.

Coach Casey exploded.

"Damn it, Hollister! I'm tired of your shit! If you taunt the offense like that on Friday night, they'll flag us for unsportsmanlike conduct."

"Sorry, coach."

"Duh," muttered somebody from the scout offense.

"Knock it off!" Casey yelled. "All of you. Quit the damn foolery and play football!"

Before Kai took his position behind Morris, he looked over the offensive formation. There were two wide receivers on the right that he knew would not fool anyone who had been watching the Foothill game film and had figured out that over eighty percent of their plays were running plays.

But Hollister did what almost any team captain would do who had not paid attention to the Foothill game film and didn't remember what his coach had told him. He yelled, "Overload left, overload left!" and the defense shifted to a wider spread.

Hollister didn't stop there with his commentary. He continued his rant against the right guard. "Meloni, I'm gonna chop your ass up for spaghetti and meatballs!"

He barely got the words out when Angelo Rodriguez took the snap under center, faked to Jerry Morris, and handed off to Kai who ran up to the line and found the hole clogged by a defensive lineman who unexpectedly shifted to the left. Kai ran into the big lineman, and instead of trying to push his way through, he spun around out of his grasp and sprinted wide to the right, picking up thirty yards before being pushed out of bounds by the safety.

Kai had expected a pat on the back from both coaches when he returned to the huddle, but he found that Coach Casey was not at all happy after he had looked at the play on Wally Prince's clipboard.

"Run the damn play the way it's shown on the diagram!" Casey said to Kai. "You're here to teach the defense how to defend Foothill, not show off!"

Kai threw a glance at Angelo who shrugged. He thought that in a real game, the running back would have done exactly what he did, but he didn't tell that to the coach. It was not a good idea to piss off a coach—even though he was dead wrong.

Casey left the huddle and Prince held up the clipboard. "Okay. We're going to do it again, except off the left side. Does everybody understand? Moore takes the ball through the hole on the left side this time."

The team nodded and Prince turned his attention to Kai. "Moore, this time, don't be so creative. Run the play the way it's diagrammed."

Prince left the huddle.

Angelo tapped Kai on the shoulder. "See what I mean when I told you about being a first string tackling dummy? They want you to fall down for Hollister."

"Bullshit," Kai muttered.

The scout team broke from the huddle on a clap and set up in formation. They were met by a barrage of catcalls from Hollister.

"I know you're coming, Moore, I know you're coming! You're all mine. You better hold onto your cornpone ass with both hands because I'm going to rip it right off!"

Kai, who had no idea what a cornpone ass was, took the ball from Angelo with Morris leading the blocking. The defensive line tried to stuff the hole between the left guard and left tackle but left some daylight when a defensive lineman was thrown off balance. Kai had no choice but to try bulling his way through the player. He charged into him and knocked him into the path of Hollister who was rushing forward to meet the threat. As Kai darted to the left, Hollister tripped over the lineman and rolled in front of him.

Kai's parting words to Hollister as he vaulted over him were, "Bye, bye, fat ass." He easily outran the cornerback, dodged the safety, and raced to the goal line.

But Casey was not interested in Kai. He stood over Hollister as he got up from the ground.

"Dammit, Hollister! You knew where the play was going, and you didn't even touch him! You looked like a goddamn clown!"

Hollister ignored Casey and watched Kai as he jogged back up the field with the scout team.

"I'll get him next time, though," Hollister murmured.

Angelo's comment about being a first string tackling dummy had a ring of truth about it. By the end of practice, the scout team had run thirty-six plays against the defense. Kai had carried the ball on half of those plays and every one of them was a blast through a hole or lack of a hole in the line. He also caught three passes from Angelo whose bullet-like throws were amazingly accurate. When Kai wasn't running or catching the ball, he led the blocking for Jerry Morris or Angelo Rodriguez.

By the end of practice, Kai felt as if he had been on the receiving end of a battering ram.

Even though he put out maximum effort during practice, Kai felt like he was not doing enough to become ready to play football on game day if he were called upon. So, after the second day of scrimmaging with defense, this time at half speed and no tackling, Kai asked Coach Prince if he could have a few words with the scout team.

Prince was surprised at the request, but he agreed.

After Prince left, Kai posed a hypothetical question to his teammates. "Suppose in the first ten minutes of the game next Friday night, that every starter has been injured, and we're called in to play against Foothill. Does anybody here feel like what we have been doing has prepared us to play against them?"

No one answered.

"Well, do we?" Kai yelled.

"Hell, no," Meloni said.

"It sounds like you got something on your mind," Angelo said cautiously.

"I do," Kai said.

Twenty minutes after practice ended on Wednesday, Nick Ferrentini happened to look out his office window toward the practice field. There were players still on the field in the growing darkness. He called Coach Casey into his office.

"What's going on out there?"

"This you're not going to believe."

"Try me."

"That's the scout team. Both of them. Offense and defense."

"What in hell are they doing?"

"They're practicing our game plan against Foothill."

"What? Who in hell authorized that?"

"Wally Prince. He's out there with them."

"This was his idea?"

"No. It was that new kid, Moore. He talked both scout teams into doing it."

Later that night, two young fighters, wearing headgear, were sparring in the ring at Mickie's Fight Club. Detective Sid Conners, a crumpled cigar in his mouth and wearing a gun in a shoulder holster over a white short-sleeved shirt, yelled at one of the fighters. "Dammit Edwards, keep your hands up! You're going to get your head knocked off if you keep doing that shit!"

At the far end of the gym, Lamont Jamison, in work-out gear and sweating profusely, paused from the bag he was pounding and watched for a few minutes. He would be fighting Edwards in a few days and wanted to see how good the boy was.

After watching Edwards for a few minutes, Lamont was convinced that he would have no trouble with him in the ring and made his way down the hallway to the lockers. Halfway down the dingy hallway, a long black arm jumped out of nowhere, grabbed Lamont by the arm, and pulled him into a dark storage room that smelled of a mixture of ammonia and an odor that Lamont had never experienced before.

The door slammed shut, throwing the room into darkness. A moment later, the light was thrown on, and Lamont found that his eyes were on the same level as someone's chest. He looked up and saw Thurman Adams looking down at him.

Lamont took a deep breath and said, "Damn it, Thurman, you scared the dawg crap out of me! What'chu doin' here, man? Conners' down on the floor! He's lookin' for you!"

"I'm lookin' for Moore. Do you know where he is?"

"Are you crazy, man? Conners' out there and he's got a gun."

"So do I." Thurman pulled out a revolver from under his jersey and slammed its four-inch barrel into Lamont's chest.

"I don't give no shit about Conners! Where's Moore?" Thurman screamed, showering spit on Lamont's face.

Lamont, terrified at the violence in Thurman's voice, held up a hand. "I heard he's playin' football again."

"At that school across the freeway?"

"I dunno know. I just heard a boy say he gonna be playin' football again. I don't keep track of them things."

Thurman backed away and looked Lamont up and down. "What boy told you this?"

"A boy on the street. I don't know his name."

"You hear anything else, you let me know? You hear?"

"I will, Thurman."

"You go out and make sure Conners' not out there."

Lamont walked out of the hallway. For just a second, he thought about telling Conners that Thurman was in the storage room. He decided against it. He needed to get the hell out of there.

Chapter Thirteen

Practice on Thursday at Jefferson Heights was less than an hour and began within a half hour after school let out. There was a reason for this. The team was being treated to a steak dinner at the Meyers' residence at 7:00 p.m. that evening.

Kai wondered why the team even bothered to suit up. After a light work-out, the remainder of the practice only involved the starting offense who were practicing their game plan and special teams who were at the far end of the field. He heard someone call his name and turned to see Paul Bishop, the wide receiver and designated kick-off returner, approaching him.

"Coach Prince needs you down at the end of the field."

Kai didn't ask why. He headed downfield and found Coach Prince watching a punt returner who bobbled the ball and then dropped it as he was rushed by two players.

Prince turned to Kai. "You run the ball fairly well. Have you ever been on a kick-off return team?"

"Yes."

"In a game?"

"Yes."

"Get out on the field with Bishop. We're going to run through a few kick-off returns. I want to see what you can do."

In the next twenty minutes, Kai competed with Paul Bishop to see who could make the most catches on a kick-off return. Even though Bishop had dropped the ball twice, they were tied at seven when practice ended.

The street leading up to the circular drive in front of the Meyers' house was so narrow that a school bus could not navigate it, so the team was brought up by three white vans that had to make several runs to get the varsity team up the hill.

Kai had never seen a place like the mansion. The short driveway on the property was twice as wide as the street and led to a circular drive lined with expensive cars. The landscape was lush, almost jungle-like in contrast to the brown grass in the flats beyond the freeway. A huge banner was over the massive front door that read, THE J. H. BOOSTERS WELCOME THE RED RAIDERS.

Kai got out of the van, followed by Angelo and six other players. He stopped and looked around. The only time he had seen a place like this was in the movies, and he wondered about the people who lived there, not making the connection between Red Meyers and the Meyers who lived in this house. He could hear loud band music coming from the backyard.

When Kai got around to the back of the house, he found that the pre-season football booster party was in full swing around a large Olympic-size pool. The music was a fast jazzy piece that came from a recording of the Jefferson Heights marching band. Across the pool, a dozen cheerleaders shook and bounced to the music as the arriving players formed a line for steaks being cooked on three outdoor grills.

The area behind the house was large and had been cut out of the hillside. Above them loomed a massive rocky shelf, and Kai wondered if any part of the rock face had ever fallen down on anyone.

Kai and Angelo got into line behind Buster Hollister, Oliver Brown, and Moose Basich, the guard on the left side. Kai looked around, ignoring the conversation of the three players in front of him. He saw Coach Ferrentini and Coach Casey, cocktails in hand, talking to several men across the swimming pool. Most of the men were dressed casually but one of them was wearing a suit. Kai nudged Angelo who was listening to the conversation of the three boys in front of him.

"Who's the suit talking to Ferrentini?" Kai asked.

"That's Joe Meyers. He owns this place."

Kai suddenly made the connection. "Red Meyer's dad?"

Angelo nodded and pointed at the three boys in front of him. He leaned over and whispered, "Listen to this brilliant conversation."

"What Casey actually said was that I could get called a fifteen-yard penalty for taunting the offense," Buster Hollister said.

"Whaaat?" Basich retorted. "Why should we get penalized fifteen yards for teaching someone to bust a football, dude?"

Oliver Brown shook his head. "We've been through this crap before. He said taunting the offense."

"But why should we get a fifteen-yard penalty for doing that?"

Angelo butted in. "The coach said taunting, t-a-u-n-t-i-n-g — not taughting — if there ever was such a word. He was not talking about teaching anything. He was talking about a penalty for unsportsmanlike conduct."

The three boys turned and stared at Angelo as if he just landed in a spaceship.

"Rodriguez," Basich said, "we already know you're a smart ass. I'd rather be playing first-string offense than a third-rate quarterback that knows how to spell. So, butt out!"

Kai and Angelo took their steaks to a long table alongside the pool where the team was sitting. After they sat down, Kai leaned over to Angelo and whispered, "What do these people up here do for a living?"

"Do you mean in general?"

"Yes."

"Everybody has money up here, except for that area around the school and north of the freeway. The Meyers own a Jaguar dealership. Tyler Jefferson's dad owns a dental practice with a dozen locations. But he really made his money selling off land. This entire area around us used to be one huge cattle ranch, and Tyler's great-grandpa owned it. That's why they call it Jefferson Heights."

Kai looked at Angelo sharply. "Did you say that Meyer's dad owns a Jaguar dealership?"

"Yeah, why?"

The first thing that Kai did when he got on campus the next morning was to head to the field house to see the starting line-up for that night's game against Foothill. He turned when he heard the clatter of heels behind him and saw Patty Jefferson from his Journalism class approaching him. She wore a short skirt and an oversize red and white sweater with the words, 'Red Raiders' embroidered on it.

"Hey, Kai. What's up?"

"Going inside to see the starting line-up."

Patty didn't pay much attention to his answer. She stopped and pulled her sweater over her head, revealing a diaphanous, tight-fitting blouse. She saw Kai watching and smiled coyly.

Kai turned and started walking, rolling his eyes in disbelief.

Patty bounced alongside him, chatting about the weird girls in the Journalism class. She sounded differently than in class where she kept her voice down. Out here, her voice tingled with excitement. She sounded like a kid opening a Christmas present.

For a moment, Kai wondered if she was on bennies, but his thoughts were interrupted when he saw a Jaguar sports car parked in Ferrentini's spot in front of the field house.

On the license plate frame of the Jaguar were printed the words, MEYERS IMPORTS.

"What are *you* doing, bro?" Patty said as she came to a stop alongside him. She was standing so close that he could smell her breath. It smelled of peppermint.

Kai didn't like being called 'bro'. He shook his head and looked at this marvelous creature whose only apparent defect appeared to be in her brain. He had to admit that she was an astonishingly beautiful girl.

"Meyers' Imports?" Kai said. "That's Red Meyers dad, isn't it?"

Patty smiled. "It sure is. That's one of the perks of being *duh* head coach in *duh* Heights. You get a neat car."

Kai felt she was too damn close for comfort and stepped back. He found it hard to keep his eyes off that tight-fitting blouse. Kai looked down to keep from staring, but there were those long bare legs down there that were just as tempting. He gave up and looked up into her eyes.

They were a sparkling bright green.

Damn, Kai thought, *I bet her farts smell like peppermint too.*

"And I would guess that Ferrentini probably gets his teeth capped by Tyler's dad," Kai remarked sarcastically.

"Why shouldn't he? My dad is a great dentist and just about everybody here goes to see him."

Kai was astonished. "Tyler is your brother?"

"Unfortunately, yes, but I don't really believe that. He is so uncool. I mean I think my parents adopted him." She paused for a moment and then blurted out excitedly. "You know all the girls think Tyler is *duh* bomb. But all he's hung with is a little ole firecracker. No one believes me when I tell them that it's that teeny!" She held up her pinky.

"I believe you," Kai said. He turned and walked into the field house, expecting Patty to follow him.

She didn't.

Kai found the starting roster for the game against Foothill posted on a bulletin board next to Coach Ferrentini's office in the Joseph and Anna Meyers Field House. It showed the starting line-up for offense, defense, kick-off return, and punt return teams. Red Meyers was listed on all of them except for defense.

Kai was not listed on any of them.

"Well, what in hell did you expect?" Kai murmured to himself as he walked out of the field house. "I don't own no Jag dealership."

Chapter Fourteen

Jefferson Heights versus Foothill at Home

The Jefferson Heights football team was greeted with a slowly rising cheer when the crowd saw them trotting from the field house. The cheer rose to a roar as the team entered the stadium and then bunched up at the south end of the track. They wore shiny white helmets with red trim that glistened under the stadium lights, and their uniforms, white jerseys with scarlet pants, were brand new.

Kai, wearing number 27, looked around, saw the crowd, the pageantry of the band and the spirit squad, and held back a smile.

Ferrentini raised his hand and the team ran onto the field, led by cart-wheeling cheerleaders as the booming voice of the announcer echoed across the stadium.

"Ladies and gentlemen, the Red Raiders of Jefferson Heights!"

The audience cheered, drowning out the booming of the band, as the Red Raiders swarmed onto the field.

Minutes later, Foothill had won the toss but deferred their choice to the second half. Kai took his place on the sideline alongside Angelo Rodriguez and both watched anxiously as Red Meyers and wide receiver Paul Bishop took their positions to receive the kick-off.

The ball was kicked, and Meyers caught the ball the three-yard line, ran up the center, then cut to the right, and raced to the twenty-yard line before he was tackled.

The crowd rose its feet, cheering loudly.

Angelo turned to Kai. "Did you say something?"

Kai shook his head.

He did say something, but Angelo didn't hear it. Under his breath, he had murmured, "I could have done better than that."

Much later in the game, the band was playing, and the crowd had settled down. Kai watched dejectedly as the Jefferson Heights team broke out of the huddle. He looked at the scoreboard on the south end of the field.

Jefferson Heights was leading Foothill 49 to 0. They were in the third quarter with three minutes left to go.

Kai turned to Angelo. "Do you think they'll let us in for a couple of plays at the end of the game?"

Angelo laughed. "Not a chance. They want Red to break the rushing record. They won't let us play even if we totally annihilated Foothill."

On the field, Tyler handed off to Red Meyers who was tackled for a loss of two yards. Ferrentini waved Red over to the sideline and began yelling at him. Meyers took off his helmet and was yelling back at Ferrentini.

Kai watched the exchange of words for a few seconds and then turned to Angelo. "What in the hell is going on?"

"Our illustrious running back has a nasty habit of changing a pass play in the huddle because he wants to run the ball. Ferrentini usually lets it go, but when Red calls a bummer, he gets pissed."

"Are you kidding me?"

Angelo smiled and said, "Fraid not."

"I never heard of a running back changing a play. It's usually the quarterback who does that."

"Not here. Red has a lot of influence on this team. Tyler listens to him because Red seems like he has an uncanny sense of knowing what the defense is going to do."

Kai started to say something in response but stopped himself. He remembered what Father Mike had said in the car when he showed him the high school campus for the first time. Things were definitely different here in the Heights.

Later in the game with the scoreboard showing Jefferson Heights 70 and Foothill 3 with three seconds on the clock, Kai, helmet on and standing alone on the sideline, kicked the turf aimlessly. A few minutes earlier, it was announced that Red Meyers had run for two hundred and eighty yards and needed seven hundred more for the State record. In response to the announcement, the Foothill coach ripped off his headset and threw his playbook on the ground.

Kai, his uniform embarrassingly clean, absentmindedly looked toward the stands. He saw Edna McKay standing seven rows up, a look of concern on her face. For the first time since he started school in Jefferson Heights, Kai remembered his mother and what had happened to her.

The Jefferson Heights offense stayed in the huddle as time ran out. The horn sounded and the game was over. The team celebrated by rushing onto the field.

Kai joined them, not wanting to be seen standing alone on the sideline. It was then that he saw something he had never seen on a football field.

The Foothill coach ordered his team to get on the buses and turned his back on Ferrentini when he tried to shake his hands.

Ferrentini then made the mistake of calling after him. "Good sportsmanship, Ken. Isn't that what we're supposed to be teaching our boys?"

The Foothill coach spun around, his face florid with anger. "What in hell do you know about sportsmanship, Ferrentini? What have you gained by humiliating us? Do they pay you up here by the number of points you rack up?"

The Foothill coach turned and walked away before Ferrentini could respond.

By the time, Kai reached the field house, his disappointment turned into anger at not being able to play. Instead of going to the dressing room, he headed down the hallway toward Ferrentini's office.

Coach Prince saw the look on his face and stopped him.

"Where are you going?"

"To see Ferrentini."

"You can't see him right now, not with that look on your face. Tell me what you want to talk to him about."

"I don't want to talk to you. I want to talk to Ferrentini."

"First of all," Prince said patiently, "he's *Coach* Ferrentini. Don't ever call him by his last name like you just did. But let me tell you something else. Coach Ferrentini doesn't talk to players about assignments. If you walked into his office, he would've humiliated you."

"All I wanted was to ask him for some playing time."

"Bullshit! You would've done nothing but piss him off, and he would've thrown you out of his office."

Kai looked away.

"Listen Moore. You'll get your chance. You're a good athlete and you know what you're doing. Do what you do every day on the practice field, and you will get your chance."

Kai turned to face Prince. "Do you really believe that? Because I don't. Ferrentini kept first string in even when we were up by seventy. That ain't right. I've never seen any coach do that before . . . and I've never seen a high school coach drive a Jaguar either."

"Listen, Moore, you don't have a clue as to what's going on here. Meyers is seven hundred yards away from the rushing record, and that's why he plays. We want that record for the school. Don't you understand that?"

Prince reached out and put his hand on Kai's shoulder.

"Look, I'll do my best to get you some playing time. Okay?"

Kai walked back to the locker room and took a shower before getting dressed and walking home. He remembered that he had an assistant coach in his freshman year who had once told the team that one of these days you will get married, and you will never be able to tell your wife what it feels like to be on a football field on a Friday night. If you try to, you will find her looking at you like you are from another planet, so don't even bother telling her.

But this Friday night was not a good night for Kai. He didn't get to play. It was a night he didn't want to remember.

Kai walked out of the school parking lot, alone and frustrated, forgetting that Edna McKay was waiting to drive him home. He was not happy with what had happened that night, but others were. As he headed out to the street, tires squealed as cars loaded with screaming and jubilant teenagers celebrated their victory over Foothill.

He had walked nearly a half mile along a dimly lit sidewalk in a quiet neighborhood when Edna McKay's Mercedes 450 SEL with its top-down pulled alongside him.

"Want a ride home, Kai?"

"No thanks, Mrs. McKay." Kai kept walking without turning to look at her.

Edna got out of the car and hurried to catch up with him. The two of them walked silently for a moment before Edna broke the silence.

"You know," Edna said, "that if you walk home this way, you'll be passing through gang territory north of the freeway. They would love to catch a football player alone at night."

"It wouldn't be the first time I had a run-in with a gang."

"Come on back to the car. We can talk when we get home."

"You know, it wouldn't be as bad if. . . "

"If, what?"

Kai stopped, looked at her, and then looked back in the direction of the school. He looked up in the Heights. The lights of the residences in the hills sparkled like gemstones.

"It wasn't so bad when my mother was around." Kai looked at the ground and kicked a loose rock into some bushes. "I was on a winning team in every sport I played at Saint Ignatius. But things sometimes went bad there . . . really bad. Not all of the players had their heads on straight. A lot of them had family problems. Some of them were messed up with drugs. Some of them died . . . killed in a gang fight. Sometimes over nothing!"

Kai paused again and began walking back to where Edna had parked her Mercedes. "I had an advantage. My advantage was the difference for me. It was my mother. She said that if everyone worked to do their best every day and didn't worry so much about the past, the world would be a better place. But now I wonder if she had any clue about what was goin' on in the real world."

He clenched his fists and continued. "I killed two of the gangbangers that killed her. I'm not sorry that I did that. I'd do it again. If Thurman Adams were here right now, I'd kill him too."

"Kai, you can't mean that."

"I do," Kai said firmly.

They walked silently for a minute before Edna said anything in response.

"Kai, you talked about your mother. What do you think she would tell you about your feelings for these people?"

"I know what she would say."

"And what was that?"

"She would tell me to stop hating so much."

"And that," Edna said, "would be very good advice."

That same night on the outskirts of downtown Los Angeles, Saint Ignatius beat San Sebastian High School to in a hard-fought game.

Thurman Adams tried to get onto the school grounds to see if Ryan Moore was playing, but there were four off-duty police officers checking every car and person entering the school grounds that night. He could get a haircut and wear a pin-striped suit, but there was nothing he could do to change the look in those hate-filled eyes. There was no way that Thurman Adams could get past those cops.

So, he went back to the warehouse and asked Lucy to come with him. When she asked where they were going, Thurman told her she was going to see a football game.

"I don't like football!" she protested.

"You don't have to watch the game. I just want to find out if Ryan Moore is playing tonight."

"And how am I supposed to do that?"

"Ask around."

When they arrived at the entrance to the Saint Ignatius parking lot, Thurman gave Lucy a ten-dollar bill and told her what she needed to do. He would be waiting for her on the bus bench across from the entrance to the school.

Lucy came out thirty minutes later with a cherry snow cone in one hand and a program in the other. She crossed the street and sat down next to Thurman.

"They say he's not playing tonight. He's not in school anymore."

"Who's saying that?"

"The girls I talked to."

"Maybe they lyin'."

"They ain't lying, Thurman. I got a program. His picture's not in it." She handed the program to Thurman.

Thurman opened it to the section that had the photos of the Saint Ignatius players. He took his time studying each of the pictures. When he was done, he said, "He's not playing."

"That's what I told you," Lucy said. "Why don't you listen to me?"

Thurman looked across the street at the high school. "How many schools are there like this in this City."

Lucy shrugged.

"He's playin' somewhere," Thurman said. "Maybe, we go to a different school next Friday night."

"There's too many schools in the County. You're not going to find him doing that."

"How do you know that?"

"Look at the back of that program."

Thurman did so. There was a schedule for all high school football games that were to be played in Los Angeles County next Friday night. There were thirty-three of them.

Chapter Fifteen

On Monday evening, the scout team had just finished full speed practice that involved running the plays that North Hills was expected to use this coming Friday night. Kai trotted off the field to jog with Angelo when he heard Coach Prince calling him.

"Moore, where do you think you're going?"

Kai and Angelo stopped and turned around.

"To jog a bit, coach," Kai said. "I thought we were done."

Coach Prince paused for effect, a little smile on his face.

"Punt returners have to stay to practice with special teams."

Kai looked confused. "What?"

"If you do well in practice, you will take over for Meyers this Friday on punt returns."

Kai looked at Angelo who nodded in affirmation.

"Way to go," Angelo said.

The game Friday night was scheduled to be played at North Hills High School, a twenty-minute bus ride on the freeway to the east. Earlier that morning, Kai had stopped by the field house and checked the starting lineup for the game. He was listed as the punt returner. It was a small but important part of the game. But there was also another change. Another player had replaced Red Meyers on the kick-off return team.

During practice, Coach Prince had listed several rules that a punt returner on the Jefferson Heights football team needed to observe Kai already knew. Rules like letting a punt go that fell into the space between the goal and the five-yard line when you had opposing players on top of you, and the obvious ones: never run backward after catching a ball, don't try catching a ball over your shoulder, and whatever you do, don't fumble.

But Prince had also set a goal for a punt return that was not fair caught. The goal was ten yards, equivalent to a first down. Kai knew that it was not completely up to him to do that. He also needed good blocking.

Jefferson Heights versus North Hills at North Hills

Things didn't go well for Red Meyers that night, starting with the first play Jefferson Heights had the ball. Tyler Jefferson pitched the ball to Red only to have a huge defensive lineman named Michaels slice through the line and hit Red like a battering ram.

Michaels held Red to the ground by his shoulder pads and yelled at him in a voice that could be heard from the Jefferson Heights sideline.

"Welcome to North Hills, golden boy. You ain't breaking any State record on this here football field tonight."

Using a fist on Red's chest, Michaels pushed himself up and began walking away. Red still on the ground retaliated by kicking him in the leg. The big defensive lineman turned and kicked Red in the thigh.

Red leaped to his feet, his fists cocked.

Two football officials raced in and separated the two fuming players.

Seven minutes into the game, North Hills had the ball with fourth and fifteen on their thirty-five-yard line and sent in their punt team. Coach Prince ordered the Jefferson Heights punt return team onto the field.

Kai took up a position on the Jefferson Heights forty-yard line. Excited at being in the game, Kai bounced on his toes while waiting for the punt.

Unexpectedly, the punter kicked a boomer, sending the ball over Kai's head. Kai sprinted downfield, circled under the ball, and caught it at the twenty-five-yard line, breaking Coach Prince's rule of never catching a punt over your shoulder.

Kai turned and sprinted diagonally toward the Jefferson Heights' sideline. The North Hills players changed direction to intercept him.

He raced upfield along the sideline behind three teammates who formed a rolling screen. Nearly half of the North Hills team converged seconds later and rolled into the Jefferson Heights players like over-sized bowling balls. Kai was so close to the pileup that he was unable to avoid the tangled mess of flying bodies. He tried to vault over the players, but someone grabbed his foot while he was in the air, and he lost his balance. He hit the ground hard and rolled several times before coming to a stop.

The players slowly got up from the pile. Kai pulled a clod of turf out of his facemask, rubbed his ribs, and rose to his feet.

Red Meyers ran past Kai as he trotted off-field. "Not as easy as it looks, eh!"

Kai resisted an urge to grab him by the jersey and lay a fist into his mouth.

Four minutes into the third quarter, Jefferson Heights was leading North Hills 7 to 3 with Jefferson Heights in possession of the ball. An exhausted Red Meyers broke out of the huddle and took up a position three yards behind Tyler Jefferson. He had taken a pounding by the defense who seem intent on destroying him. His cockiness dissolved into fear when he saw Michaels grinning at him from the other side of the scrimmage line.

It wasn't only the size of the defensive lineman that bothered Red. It was his speed and eagerness to do as much damage as he could while making a tackle. The fact that Red had Jerry Morris as a blocking back made no difference. Michaels ran right through him.

Red took the hand-off from Tyler on the option play and was buried again by Michaels.

Coach Ferrentini decided that now was the time to go to a passing game.

That didn't work against North Hills either.

Twenty-two minutes later, there were fourteen seconds left in the game and the clock was running out with neither team being able to stop it.

The score was Jefferson Heights 10, North Hills 6.

Jefferson Heights took their time in the huddle while the North Hills' defensive unit watched in frustration.

The horn blared ending the game. Jefferson Heights had won . . . just barely.

Coach Ferrentini and his coaches were not happy with the performance of the Red Raiders that night. It was a quiet ride on the bus back to Jefferson Heights.

Kai knew they would be spending a lot of time in the locker room listening to the coaches before they would be released, but he was relatively happy. He had done well in his first appearance for the Jefferson Heights Red Raiders. He had made a return on four of the seven times the ball had been punted to him and had gained a total of fifty-seven yards, easily meeting Coach Prince's goal of ten yards a return. On the other hand, Red Meyers had run the ball twenty-six times and had gained a total of twenty-one yards.

North Hills had a strong defensive unit, but Kai felt he could have done a better job at running the ball than Red Meyers. He began thinking he might have a shot at taking over his position.

Thurman Adams figured that if anybody knew where Ryan Moore had gone, it would be the principal of Saint Ignatius High School. There was a narrow side street behind the high school campus that had little traffic, and he had no problem climbing over the wall into the school grounds.

The one thing that Thurman Adams had in his favor was persistence and with persistence came patience. He waited in the darkness alongside the new field house for over an hour so that he could determine the pattern of the security officer who walked the grounds.

Once he learned that the guard walked the grounds once an hour on the half hour, he waited until the guard was at the back of the property before he made his move. He broke a window to get into the main school building and quickly found the principal's office.

The room was dark, and Thurman didn't want to run the risk of turning on the light. He carried a small penlight he had stolen out of a pharmacy and used it to navigate his way around the office.

The first place he checked was the file cabinets. They contained nothing but the school's financial, fund-raising, and maintenance records. He went to a large ornate desk made of dark wood. Holding the penlight between his teeth, he began pulling out drawers one by one. When he didn't find what he was looking for in a drawer, he threw it and its contents across the room, not giving a damn that the security guard might hear the noise. If the security guard happened to hear the noise, Thurman had a gun to take care of that problem, and no one would even hear the gunshot from outside the school.

In the middle drawer of the desk, he found some loose cash, about ten dollars' worth. The drawer also contained a personal checkbook. He put the money in his pocket and threw the checkbook across the room, knocking a statute of Jesus off the wall.

In the top desk drawer on the right, he found something he thought might be helpful. It was the priest's address book. He put the address book in his pocket, hoping that it might contain an address where Ryan Moore was living.

Chapter Sixteen

On the Saturday morning after the North Hills game, Kai was awakened when he heard the murmuring of voices and the sound of pots and pans clanking from a distant part of the house. He listened for a beat and then swung out of bed.

He groaned loudly and held his ribs as pain surged through them, the result of a hard tackle the night before. He fought off the pain and put on a T-shirt and shorts.

When he walked into the kitchen, he found Edna McKay frying bacon and eggs. Two men were at the table with coffee mugs in front of them. One was Father Mike McKay. The other man looked a little bit like him.

"Hi Kai, how are you doing?" Father Mike said.

Kai looked at Edna who had turned away from the stove, to the stranger sitting at the table, and then back to Father Mike.

"I'm fine," Kai replied. "What's goin' on?"

"Kai, this is my younger brother, Franklin McKay," Father Mike said.

Franklin McKay got up and extended his hand across the table to Kai.

They shook hands.

"That was a nice performance you put on last night," Franklin said.

"You saw the game?" Kai said.

"I did."

"They came close to beating us."

"We won, though. That's what counts if we want to be in contention for the championship."

The use of the word 'we' puzzled Kai. Why would Father Mike's brother attend a high school football game?

"You look familiar to me," Kai said.

"How about at school?"

"You a teacher?"

Father Mike answered the question. "Franklin is the principal at Jefferson Heights. How do you think I got you in there?"

Kai looked embarrassed.

"Why don't you sit down, Kai, and join us?" Franklin said.

"I'm sorry I didn't recognize you, Mr. McKay."

"No problem. I'm as new in Jefferson Heights as you are."

The doorbell rang.

"That'll be Sid," Father Mike said, as he got up and headed for the door.

Kai settled himself into the chair. Seconds later, Father Mike returned with Sid Conners.

Kai smiled when he saw Conners and got up. "Now, I know this is bad news!"

"How are you doin', champ?" Conners said as he looked Kai over. "Looks like you're spending some serious time in the weight room. When are you comin' back to fight for me?"

Conners assumed a fighter's pose. Kai shook his head in warning. Conners' hands came down quickly when he realized that his actions had created an awkward moment.

Later, all five of them were at the table eating breakfast with Kai wondering what was going on. First of all, Father Mike and his brother showed up and then unexpectedly Sergeant Sid Conners. Kai looked at Conners and noticed it was the first time he had seen Conners without his shoulder holster and gun.

Father Mike was the first person to break the ice, but it wasn't about the reason why they were gathered here.

"Did you get to play much last night?" Father Mike asked.

Kai set down his fork and wiped his face with a napkin. "I played a little on punt return. North Hills was real tough. They had me covered pretty well."

"He picked up twenty-six yards on one carry," Edna said.

"Twenty-six yards won't get anyone a college scholarship," Kai said.

It was silent for a few moments. He looked around the table and saw everyone was staring at him. "What's goin' on?"

Conners leaned on the table with his elbows. "Your ole pal, Thurman Adams, paid a visit to Mickie's gym a few days ago."

"Okay."

"He asked about you. Wanted to know where you're livin'. And that's not the worst of it. He was carrying a piece."

All eyes were on Kai as he nodded in response to what Conners said without any show of emotion.

"And someone broke into the school early this morning and trashed my office," Father Mike added. "The only thing missing was a little money and my address book. Sid thinks it was Adams who did it."

"Adams won't be able to read anything in that book," Conners interjected. "He can't read, and he doesn't even know how to drive." He turned toward Kai. "But that won't stop him. In his mind, you wrecked his chance to get out of the ghetto and he wants payback."

"Payback for what?" Edna asked. "What did Kai do to him?"

"Thurman got this idea that he could make money as a prizefighter," Conners said. "The problem was that he only had two weeks of training, and he didn't belong in no ring. I agreed to match him up with Kai because I thought he was the only fighter that I had that was responsible enough not to hurt him. I also told Kai to take it easy on him."

"What happened?"

"Kai didn't follow my advice."

"I had no choice," Kai said. "The fight was over. I knocked him down, but he came after me and I had to defend myself."

"This boy here hit Adams several times and laid him out on the canvas with a vicious hook," Conners added. "Thurman has never been able to get over that."

Edna McKay was incredulous. "You mean this guy killed Kai's mother because he got a whippin' in a boxing match?"

"That's about it in a nutshell," Conners replied.

"If Adams doesn't know how to drive," Father Mike asked, "how can he get out here?"

Conners shrugged. "He can find someone to drive him. But he'll have one helluva time cruising around out here without being spotted. And it ain't just because he's Black. He's one scary-lookin' dude. The only way I think Adams can get to Kai is when he's playin' football. If I were you, I would rethink this whole idea about him playing football."

"Wait a minute!" Kai said in a raised voice. "Are you tellin' me that I should give up football?"

"You know what the guy is like. He's crazy!"

Kai looked around the table before his eyes settled back on Conners. "I'm not givin' up football, Sergeant Conners. I hope Adams does come out here because I've got a score to settle with him."

Edna McKay held up a hand and looked at Father Mike. "Wait a minute. I have a question. Was my address in the book that was taken?"

"Unfortunately, it was," Father Mike replied.

"But Sergeant Conners, you said he couldn't read."

"I did," Conners replied. "But that doesn't mean he can't find somebody who does."

"Let me ask a question, Sid," Father Mike said. "You seem to know this kid fairly well. Does he have the smarts to be able to track down where Kai is living just because my mom's name is in the address book?"

"You can never be sure."

"But you said he couldn't drive," Edna said.

"Same answer. Nevertheless, I happen to think Thurman's best shot at finding Kai is on the football field."

"So, what do we do?" Edna asked.

"Let me play football," Kai said firmly.

They all looked at him.

"Let him come out after me. I'll be waiting for him," Kai added.

"But, Sergeant Conners says he's got a gun," Edna pointed out.

"So, do I," Conners said, "and I know how to use it."

"But what if your theory is right?" Father Mike asked Conners. "Suppose this guy comes after Kai while he's in a game?"

"Are we all on the same page here?" Conners asked. "If we are, I can tell you this. I know what Thurman looks like. If Kai decides to play football, I will be at every game with two uniformed teams as backup. If Thurman shows up, we'll be able to spot him before he does anything."

The decision was made that Kai would stay in the football program. Conners assured them he would be covering every game with two teams of uniformed police officers. Franklin McKay said that his entire security force was already on campus during home games, but that he would add two additional security officers that traveled with the football team on away games.

When Kai went back to his room after Conners left, he began thinking that maybe he needed to do something about Thurman. The first thing he needed to do was to get hold of a gun. The second thing he had to do was to find Thurman Adams.

After he finished doing his homework, Kai had changed into his running gear and was walking down the hallway when he heard a familiar tune coming from somewhere in the house. Edna McKay liked 60's music and one of her favorite songs, *Crystal Blue Persuasion* by Tommy James and the Shondells, was playing softly.

He was certain the music was coming from Edna's bedroom. Just as he walked past her room, he heard a soft clicking sound, like metal on metal, that also sounded familiar. He froze. He didn't want to go back and see what she was doing, but curiosity got the best of him. He looked through the half-open door into her room.

Edna was stooped over an end table and loading cartridges into a .38 revolver. She slapped the cylinder shut and put the gun back into the drawer of the end table.

Kai tiptoed down the hall toward the front door. As he walked outside, he thought that what he saw in Edna's bedroom lent a whole new meaning to the title of the song *Crystal Blue Persuasion*. When he began jogging down Driskell, he realized he now knew where he could get a gun.

Chapter Seventeen

Jefferson Heights versus Walnut Hills at Home

At the top of the bleachers on the Walnut Hills side of the field, Sid Conners leaned against the back rail and scanned the crowd with binoculars. Next to him, a bored uniformed policeman turned and looked down at several girls heading for the snack shack behind the bleachers.

Conners also turned and looked down, thinking that the officer had seen something. All he saw was a line in front of the snack shack and a group of three girls chatting near the restrooms.

"What do you have?" Conners asked.

"Nothing," the officer said.

"Well, you sure as hell won't see him coming out of the girl's restroom," Conners said sarcastically. "I don't think Adams is into cross-dressing."

The officer grunted in response.

Conners looked up into the hills. It was beautiful out here at night, the lights from the homes up in the hills looked like ringlets of a diamond tiara. A fresh breeze was sliding around the hill from the west. It would be a pleasant place to live, Conners thought.

But then he thought of Thurman Adams and wondered what he might do to take advantage of the situation if he were here. The nearest street up in the hills would be an ideal place for a sniper. A person who knew how to use a rifle with a scope could easily take out someone on the football field.

Conners doubted that Adams had the experience or skill necessary to do something like that. Nevertheless, he decided that after the game, he needed to check out the street above them to see if it was a good place where a sniper could take up a position.

His attention was diverted back to the football field when he heard the referee blow the whistle to start the next play.

Midway through the first half, Walnut Hills was getting into punt formation at the fifty-yard line. Kai was already in position at the twenty-five-yard line to receive the football when he heard Coach Prince calling his name.

He turned to look. The Coach signaled him to move back five more yards and he did so, but not before he caught a glimpse of Red Meyers on the sideline glaring at him. Kai turned his attention back to the field and nervously bounced on his toes, awaiting the punt.

The ball was kicked but fell alarmingly short. Kai ran toward the ball hoping to catch it on the bounce. A second before he reached the ball, he heard Coach Ferrentini yelling to let it go, but it was too late. The ball was already in his hands.

He looked up and saw why Ferrentini had been yelling at him. Most of the Walnut Hills team was bearing down on him. Kai ran forward to meet them. He sidestepped the first player like a toreador and then sidestepped another one. He then darted to the right and gained ten more yards before he was cut down.

Inspired by the cheering crowd, Kai quickly got up. He tossed the ball to the referee and headed off the field.

He passed the Jefferson Heights' offensive unit on his way to the bench. Several of the players swatted Kai's outstretched hand. Red Meyers, however, looked away.

On the sideline, Angelo greeted Kai with a bear hug that caused Kai to wince in pain.

In the third quarter, Kai looked up at the scoreboard. Jefferson Heights was leading Walnut Hills 16 to 14 with less than four minutes in the quarter. He felt some pride in knowing that one of his punt returns put his team in field position to score, and that he was averaging sixteen yards a carry.

Kai turned to Angelo who was at his side. "Angelo, do you like playing football?"

Angelo looked at Kai like he was nuts It was the first time that Kai had seen the smile fade away.

"I'm serious, Angelo. Do you like playing football? Do you like it well enough to just stand here on the sideline watching your teammates kicking ass on the field?"

Angelo's smile returned just as quickly as it had faded. "Bro, there is no place in the world where I would rather be on a Friday night than on a football field."

Kai didn't like being called 'bro', but he said nothing. Angelo was fast becoming his best friend.

A huge cheer erupted from the Jefferson Heights fans as Red Meyers caught an over-the-shoulder pass. Meyers was immediately caught from behind by a faster runner and was tackled five yards short of the goal line.

"You know, I sort of feel the same way," Kai said to Angelo. He was thinking if he made that catch, no one would have caught him from behind. He would have scored a touchdown.

"Even if Meyers gets all the glory?" Angelo said.

"Glory? What glory? I'd be one sorry-ass dude if a little ole safety ran me down from behind."

In the fourth quarter with three minutes to go, Jefferson Heights stopped Walnut Hills on its thirty-three-yard line.

Kai took up a position to return a punt on the Jefferson Heights thirty-five-yard line and looked up at the scoreboard. Jefferson Heights was leading Walnut Hills 16 to 14. All his team had to do to win the game was to hold onto the ball for the next three minutes.

He bounced on his toes awaiting the punt return, thinking that this was one time where he had to catch the ball. If he dropped it, Walnut would have a chance at recovery. If he let it go, on the other hand, Jefferson Heights would still keep the ball. Coach Lindsey at

Saint Ignatius would have told him what to do in a situation like this, but when he looked at the sideline for instructions, Coach Prince was busy talking to Ferrentini.

Too late now.

The punter kicked the ball high, and it landed about ten yards in front of Kai and began rolling toward him. Three Walnut Hills players quickly surrounded the ball and began sidestepping while watching it roll.

The rest of the players relaxed, thinking the ball was about to be blown dead. But not one of them was paying any attention to Kai who saw an opportunity he couldn't pass up.

Kai struck as quickly as a cobra. He snatched the ball off the ground and charged through the players who were following the ball. He blasted his way through another group of unsuspecting players who thought the ball was down, and then ran over the punter, knocking him on his ass.

Seconds later, he crossed the goal line holding the ball over his head.

Chapter Eighteen

Thurman Adams sat at a counter of the rundown diner called Dodgers near the City Produce Market eating breakfast. To his right were several elderly Black men in work clothes enjoying each other's company over coffee.

The front page of the sports section of a newspaper lay on the counter next to Thurman, but he wasn't looking at it. He was halfheartedly listening to the men.

They were talking about placing a bet on a horse that was running at some racetrack in New Jersey. Thurman didn't know how they planned to place a bet in a race that was going to be held all the way across the entire country, but he knew that to place a bet on a horse, you needed money. He looked at the old men and sized them up, thinking he could take on all three of them if he had to. But it wouldn't be worth it. They probably didn't have that much money in the first place to make it worth the effort.

It was then that he looked down and noticed the newspaper lying on the counter next to him. It was opened to the sports section, and it showed a picture of a player running with the football with another player in hot pursuit. It was the eyes that caused Thurman to take notice of the picture. A flash of recognition crossed his face. He had seen those eyes before.

Thurman turned to one of the old men who was sitting a few stools away.

"Hey man!" Thurman called out.

The old man turned. He was wearing a railroad engineer's cap and bib overalls over a checked flannel shirt. "You talking to me, boy?"

"What's dis' say?" Thurman said, pointing to the picture.

The old man looked at the picture. "That's a picture. It shows a football player. You blind or somethin'?"

"What about the words under the picture, you old fool."

"Boy, I may be old, but I'm no fool. Now, if you asked me real nice, I might tell you what it say."

Thurman glared at him.

The old man sighed. He pulled a pair of bifocals out of a pocket and put them on. He spun the newspaper toward him. "It said Kai Moore, number 27, e-e-e-ludes Jason Roberts for a Jefferson Heights' touchdown in a squeaker."

"What does e-e-e-ludes mean?"

The old man looked at his friends, and they began laughing noisily.

"Man, you ain't never been to no school, have you?"

Thurman glared at him.

One of the men farther down the table spoke up. "He sure look like a dumb shit to me."

The old men laughed again.

"Are you sure that says Kai Moore? Not Ryan Moore?"

"Look here dude," the old man closest to him said, "they used to teach reading where I went to school and that was near fifty years ago."

Thurman looked off in the distance, a puzzled look on his face. Suddenly, he grabbed the newspaper and stood up.

The waitress walked up to Thurman. "Can I get you anything else?"

Thurman pulled his gun out from under his jersey and pointed it at her. "Yeah, how about cutting loose with all yo cash-money, mushroom butt?"

"Jimmie, I told you that boy was a gangster!" the old man said.

Thurman turned to the old man and shoved the gun into his ribs. "Read this, you old fool. Gimme your damn wallet before I blow your skanky ass off the stool!"

"Mister, I don't know who you are," the waitress said, "but don't you ever dare come in here again."

Without even thinking, Thurman turned and shot her. He jumped over the counter and took the money out of the cash register.

Lucy watched Thurman counting his haul later that day. "Where did you get that money."

"None of your business."

"You stole it, didn't you? Where were you this morning? Dodgers?"

"I told you, it ain't none of your business."

"You need to leave here."

"Why?"

"You're making my place too hot. How many places have you robbed in the last week? Word is out on the street. The police know who you are, and they're going to catch you. I don't want to go down with you."

Thurman nodded thoughtfully. She was right. What he did that morning was going to cause some problems.

"Where is Jefferson Heights?" he asked.

"What?"

"Jefferson Heights. Where is it?"

"It's out east somewhere."

"How do I get there?"

"Well, if you had a car, you could take the Pomona Freeway."

"I don't know how to drive. If I get you a car, will you take me?"

"No."

"Why not?"

"Ain't ridin' in a stolen car with you. Ain't going nowhere with you, anymore. Get out of here!"

Chapter Nineteen

Jefferson Heights versus Highlands at Highlands

The Jefferson Heights' offense broke out of the huddle looking as if they meant business and lined up in a tight formation on their twenty-six-yard line.

Kai looked up at the scoreboard.

Jefferson Heights was getting beaten by Highlands 10 to 7. There was little more than four minutes left in the third quarter, still plenty of time to win this ball game.

Earlier, Coach Prince had pointed out a weakness in the Highlands' defense to Kai. The cornerback closest to them was playing too far inside. Prince made the astonishing comment that it showed a lack of respect for Red Meyer's speed, leaving Kai to wonder why Prince had told him that.

Now, as Coach Prince moved closer to Ferrentini, Kai followed, thinking that the comment was a signal they might be deciding to put him in the game.

Ferrentini, clearly agitated, turned to Prince. "Does that look like a passing formation to you?"

Prince, wise enough not to answer, merely shook his head.

On the field, Red Meyers took a hand-off from Tyler Jefferson and dove for a hole off right tackle. He picked up five yards falling short of a first down by one yard.

Ferrentini, his face turning red, waved Tyler over to the hash marks. "Why da' hell did you change my play?"

"I didn't, coach! Red said you signaled Two Dive Right."

"Damn it! Time out! Where is that redheaded pissant? I want to talk to him." Ferrentini turned to Prince. "Wally, take over. Punt the damn ball."

Coach Prince smiled and signaled Kai to join him and Tyler.

"Boys, we have an opportunity to rack up big-time yardage by running a sweep to the left." He turned to Kai. "Do you remember what I said about the weakness on the left side?"

Kai nodded as he put on his helmet, realizing that he now had an opportunity to show what he could do on offense.

"Coach Ferrentini said he wanted to punt the ball!" Tyler protested.

"You heard wrong, Tyler! He said to run it . . . not punt it. Sounds almost like the same thing!"

Tyler smiled.

"Thirty-eight sweep left, thirty-eight sweep left," Prince continued. "Now get out there and get a first down!"

Despite being called to the sideline by Ferrentini, Red Meyers ignored him and headed for the bench.

Ferrentini caught up with him and spun him around by the shoulder pads.

"Tell me this, Meyers," Ferrentini said, trying to control his anger. "Who's the coach on this team?"

"I guess you think you are," Meyers said.

"You're goddamn right I am!" Ferrentini said, his face turning beet red. "You run the plays the way I call them, or you don't get to play! Do you understand?"

Red looked at Ferrentini as if he were talking to a child. "I can't break the State record if all we run are passing plays."

Ferrentini blew up. "Screw the goddamn record! The only way you're goin' to break the record is if we get into the playoffs, and the way you're running the ball, we sure as hell ain't goin' to the playoffs."

Red looked away.

"Look at me boy. I need you to tell me that you understand what I am trying to tell you."

Red looked back at him. "And you need to understand who is buttering your bread, coach."

"What the hell is that supposed to mean?"

Before Red could answer, a cheer went up from the Jefferson Heights stands, followed by several players on the sideline yelling, "Incoming, incoming."

Ferrentini turned to see one of his players being pursued by the safety and coming straight for the sideline. The safety in a desperate attempt to stop the runner lunged and pushed him out of bounds. The runner rolled and landed in front of Ferrentini's feet.

When the runner jumped to his feet, Ferrentini was astonished to see that the new kid, Kai Moore, was standing in front of him with the ball in his hand.

"First down, coach!" Kai said, smiling. He turned and headed back onto the field.

Red Meyers put on his helmet and started to follow.

"Where are you going, Meyers?" Ferrentini asked.

"Back in the game . . . coach."

"Sit down! This series belongs to Moore."

Kai rejoined the huddle and Tyler Jefferson looked at him and smiled. "You took that last handoff fairly well. Are you ready to try it again?"

"Always," Kai said, thinking this would be only the second time he took a handoff from Tyler and hoping this one would go as well as the previous one.

He needn't have worried about that.

On the next play, Tyler handed off to him. He ran up the middle, plowing through the line, dragging several defensive players with him, picking up ten yards before he went down.

When Kai rejoined the huddle, he wasn't even breathing hard.

Tyler looked at him. "Ready to try another one?"

Kai nodded, wondering how much hell Tyler was going to catch for ignoring the calls from the bench and running his own plays. Red had just been chewed out for doing the same thing.

Maybe, it was okay to change the play if it gained yardage.

On the next play, Tyler handed off to Kai in a dive off the right guard. The line was clogged, so Kai spun around and swept to the right. He churned through a defensive end coming in low attempting to make a tackle below the knees, then turned the right corner, and out-distanced the secondary for a thirty-yard race to the goal line.

Kai was greeted by his celebrating teammates in the end zone.

Jefferson Heights was now ahead of Highlands 13 to 10.

Later in the game, Jefferson Heights recovered a fumble on the kick-off to Highlands on their twenty-five-yard line.

Kai stood on the sideline, watching Ferrentini huddle with the offensive unit. Ferrentini didn't have a running back in the huddle, so he looked around. His eyes briefly alighted on Kai, but he continued looking. He then saw Red and waved him into the huddle.

There was a look of disappointment on Kai's face as he watched the first string offense jog onto the field.

Angelo came alongside Kai. "That bites!"

Kai, disappointed, nodded in agreement.

Jefferson Heights won the game 21 to 16, with the Red Raiders picking up another touchdown in the last minute by a scrambling Tyler Jefferson who couldn't find an open receiver. Kai didn't get a chance to get back into the game, but he knew Ferrentini had been thinking about it. The Coach had turned away from the field at least twice after disappointing plays and his eyes fell on Kai. But the call never came, and Kai watched the rest of the game with the satisfaction he had done his best in the time allotted to him.

The team and fans noisily celebrated the victory over Highlands as Nick Ferrentini and Wally Prince walked off the field toward the team buses.

Joe Meyers, puffing cigar smoke like a steam engine, came up from behind. "Hey Nick, I want to talk to you."

Ferrentini kept walking. "Later!"

Joe Meyers grabbed Ferrentini by an arm, and Ferrentini turned to face him.

"Don't walk away from me!" Meyers said angrily. "What was all that shit going on between you and Red?"

"Don't you ever talk to me like that!" Ferrentini said. "And don't you ever put a hand on me again!"

Prince gently laid a hand on Ferrentini's arm. "Let's go, Nick. The buses are waiting."

Ferrentini walked away, leaving Meyers angrily seething cigar smoke through his nose.

Chapter Twenty

The next Monday started out very well for Kai. In nearly every class that morning, there were several students who had said something enthusiastic about his impressive performance in the game last Friday night. He was disappointed he could not have played the rest of the game after he had scored that touchdown, because he felt he could have done more. But the main thing was that he was beginning to feel accepted at Jefferson Heights.

Later at practice that day, Ferrentini paid a surprise visit to the scout team. He joined Coaches Casey and Prince on the sideline.

"John, Wally . . . how's it going?"

Casey turned in surprise and then threw a glance at Prince before responding to Ferrentini. "Somehow, I don't think this is a social call, Nick." He then looked at Prince again. "When was the last time we saw Nick here on defense?" And then back to Ferrentini before Prince could answer. "You never come over here, Nick. What's on your mind?"

Before Ferrentini could reply, Angelo's voice echoed across the field. "Set! . . . Set!"

The coaches looked out onto the field in time to see Angelo handing off to Kai who dove for a hole off left tackle. The defensive line collapsed on him and cut him off, but Kai drove through two linemen, his feet churning, pushing them back, and then breaking free. He lowered his head and bulled his way into Hollister and knock him back three yards before Hollister grabbed him by the jersey and pulled him down on top of him.

"That kid does not back off," Casey said to Ferrentini. "I don't know anybody who consistently has the guts to tangle with Hollister like that."

When Ferrentini spoke again, his voice was so quiet that it seemed as if he was afraid that someone might hear him.

"I'm not making any changes when we're winning games."

Casey and Prince looked at each other.

"We're barely winning games," Casey said to Ferrentini. "Not like last year when we ran over every team in the league."

Ferrentini nodded. After a moment, he turned to Prince. "Send Moore over every day to get some practice taking a couple of hand-offs from Tyler just in case we need him. And while you're at it, send Rodriguez over for some snaps off Brown. We need to get him ready for next year."

"Moore has no next year," Prince said.

"I know that," Ferrentini said as he walked away.

Casey and Prince exchanged looks.

"I think we might be seeing a change sometime soon," Prince said to Casey after Ferrentini left.

"It's long overdue."

There were many extravagant and expensive homes in the hills above the school, and the home of the President of the Red Raiders Boosters, Doctor Robert Pittman, was no exception. The lights were blazing in the two-story mansion, and the circular drive was lined with expensive cars as Coach Nick Ferrentini parked his Jaguar at the front door. He was met by Doctor Pittman and his wife Rita and escorted to a large recreation room in the back where he was greeted with a standing ovation by thirty-six members of the booster club.

Ferrentini felt comfortable in this environment. After all, he had met with the boosters after every game for the last eight years. And they had treated him well.

Chairs had been set up facing a home theater system. Ferrentini took a position alongside the screen after handing off an edited disc to Mrs. Pittman who inserted it into the player. It was then that

Ferrentini noticed that Joe Meyers was absent. That was unusual. Meyers attended these meetings without fail.

Ferrentini began the meeting by announcing that there were some great plays in the game against Highlands, but that he and his assistants were not pleased with the team's overall performance. Nevertheless, there were plays where the team showed they could do better, and those were the ones he was going to be discussing tonight. He then signaled Mrs. Pittman to begin playing the disc.

It only took ten minutes to go through the plays that Ferrentini wanted the boosters to see. The final one was Tyler Jefferson scoring a touchdown against Highlands.

"And this is the one that put it away for us!" Ferrentini concluded. "This was designed as a pass play to the corner of the end zone with Phil Marley the intended receiver. Phil was knocked out of bounds and couldn't run his route, so Tyler scrambled in the opposite direction for a touchdown."

The lights came up in the room. The boosters got to their feet, applauding what they had just seen. Ferrentini was pleased with the response, but he knew he would have gotten a different result if he had shown the boosters some of the blunders the team had made during the game.

"Another excellent play by Tyler, who adapted to a broken play," Ferrentini continued when the applause died down. "He is an excellent athlete." He paused for a moment. "I don't want to sugarcoat this victory, gentlemen. We have a major problem. We beat Highlands last year by five touchdowns. Friday night, we beat them by five lousy stinking points. We actually let them get ahead of us at one point in the game. We have Fremont coming up . . . another easy game, thank God . . . and then a tough game coming up with Marshall if we get by Fremont. It's not goin' to be easy to beat Marshall. Are there any questions?"

A booster by the name of Maxwell stood up. Ferrentini knew very little about Maxwell. He knew that the man owned a large automotive body shop and that he was a pain in an ass. He always seemed to point something out about the game that made Ferrentini uncomfortable.

"Coach," Maxwell said, "what happened between you and Red Meyers during the game last week?"

Ferrentini decided to be direct and answer as succinctly as possible. "I sent in a play. He changed it without authorization, so I pulled him. It didn't hurt us. Moore went in for him and scored a touchdown."

"Well, I think it did hurt us," Maxwell said. "Red didn't run very well after that."

"Listen, if you'd been paying any attention at all this season, you'd have noticed that Meyers' running game has fallen off. He picked up only seventy-three yards against Highlands . . . seventy-three yards against the weakest sister in the League! If he doesn't get his butt in gear, he won't be breakin' any State records!"

Another booster stood up. His name was Spencer, and he was the owner of a pharmacy.

"Drugs?" he said.

There was nervous laughter from the boosters.

"What?" Ferrentini asked.

"Drugs?" Spencer repeated.

"Don't have a player by that name on the team. Anyone here have a serious question?"

Laughter broke out from the boosters.

Another booster spoke up. This one Ferrentini didn't know by name. He was elderly and wore a goatee, reminding Ferrentini of a disgraced Soviet communist by the name of Leon Trotsky.

"Will we be seeing more of Kai Moore?"

"Moore is on our punt return team. You'll see him there against Fremont. I'm thinking of putting him on kick-off return as well."

The meeting had gone quite well Ferrentini thought until he noticed Joe Meyers come through the door at the back of the room.

Meyers held his hand up. "Coach?" Meyers said, as he leaned against the door, a smug look on his face.

Here it comes, Ferrentini thought. *I am about to be ambushed.*

"Yes, Joe."

"Can you comment at all on what John Burns just said on the radio?"

"Joe, I didn't listen to his broadcast tonight, so I don't have a clue as to what that bum said."

"Well let me tell you what he said. It was quite a revelation. Burns said that the Black kid on your team . . . Kai Moore. Well, Kai Moore isn't his name. His real name is Ryan Moore. Now, I'm sure you have a good memory of how we lost the championship last year. Ryan Moore was the running back at Saint Ignatius who scored the winning touchdown against us. He celebrated that night by killing two teenagers."

Meyers paused for a moment, savoring the astonished looks of the faces of the boosters. "Coach, you've got a killer on your team. What I want to know is, what in the hell are you going to do about it?"

Thurman Adams was on the move that night. The first thing he did was to go to a gas station and steal a map of Los Angeles County. The second thing he did was to check out a gun shop that was located on Olympic Boulevard.

It took him an hour to make his way to the store, staying off the streets and using alleys when he could. When he got there, he looked inside a window and saw that the rifles were located on a stand-up rack at the rear of the store. He checked the door. It was made of solid steel, so he decided he would check out the back door.

He made his way through a parking lot to the alley. He passed a large dumpster full of cardboard as he walked down the alley toward the back of the store. Once he got there, he found another steel door.

Frustrated, he sat on a wooden crate next to the dumpster and tried to figure out how to get into the store without setting off the alarm system. Even if he had a crowbar, he doubted he could force open a steel door. He knew that the only way he could get into the store was to break a window and that would set off an alarm. He would have to get in, grab a rifle and ammo, and get out before the cops showed up.

It turned out that getting into the store was not so easy. The windows in front of the store were thick and shatterproof. He tried breaking one of them with a milk crate, but all it did was to set off an alarm.

Thurman ran back to the alley, jumped into the dumpster, and covered himself with cardboard. He waited for what seemed like an hour, but it could not have been more than fifteen minutes when a car drove by and stopped. He heard car doors opening, the sound of a police radio, voices, and then a rattling sound. A minute later, the car drove off, and it was quiet again.

Ten minutes later, Thurman climbed out of the dumpster and cautiously made his way around to the front. The only car parked in front of the shop was a Jaguar sedan. Light spilled out onto the sidewalk through an open door.

Thurman entered the shop with his revolver in his hand. He saw a short, bald man walking toward him, his head down, looking at an object in his hand. Thurman raised the gun and the man walked right into the barrel.

The man looked up in surprise. His tongue was protruding from the corner of his mouth as if he had just been licking his lips.

Thurman had no intention of shooting the man. He needed the man to help him find a rifle and the right kind of ammo, but he mistakenly concluded the man was sticking his tongue out at him, so he shot him.

But now, Thurman realized he had another problem. Someone might have heard the gunshot and called the police. He had to move fast.

Finding a rifle with a scope was the easy part. Finding the ammo for the gun was more difficult. It involved pulling box after box of cartridges off the display case and trying to see if the shells fit the gun. It didn't occur to Thurman that the caliber of the rifle was etched into the barrel. After a few minutes, he found a box of ammo that fit the gun.

He lost track of time and was reminded of that when he heard wheels screeching to a stop outside the store.

Thurman looked out the window and saw a police car pulling up to the curb. He grabbed the rifle and two boxes of cartridges and ran toward the rear of the store.

Unbolting the rear door, he ran out into the alley and looked both ways. He heard the whine of a car engine rapidly approaching in the distance. It would be only a matter of time before a police car turned into the alley.

He ran down the alley, threw the rifle in the dumpster, and jumped inside, covering himself and the rifle with cardboard.

Seconds later, a police car came roaring into the alley and stopped. Again, there was the sound of voices and the police radio.

Then silence, only occasionally interrupted by the chatter of the police radio.

Thurman waited for five minutes and then slowly rose from the dumpster until he could see the back door of the gun shop. A police car was near the rear door and no one was around it. Thurman grabbed the rifle and ammo, climbed out of the dumpster, and began running down the alley.

Chapter Twenty-One

Kai, lost in his thoughts, sat slumped in a large easy chair in Edna McKay's living room.

"Kai."

He didn't respond.

"Kai!" Edna said in a louder voice.

He jumped out of his reverie and looked up at Edna.

"They're here," Edna said.

Kai picked up his books from a coffee table and headed for the door. He stopped and then turned to look at Edna who had an anguished look on her face.

"I'll be all right, Edna. They have enough people coverin' me to stop a small army."

"I'm not afraid of that, Kai. What I'm afraid of is what all of this is going to do to you. I don't want to see you break apart because of the fuss going on at the school.

Kai shrugged. "How did they find out?"

"It was some newspaper reporter. Saw your picture from last Friday night. Thought you looked familiar, so he did some digging, and well . . ."

"And then everyone at the school went ballistic," Kai said bitterly. "Kept me out of school for a day while they tried to figure out what to do with the Black kid who killed two gang members."

Edna nodded.

"I remember when we had that talk about not hating people, Edna. Maybe someone should tell that to the people in the Heights."

He turned and walked out the door.

Two school security guards in maroon blazers waited for Kai outside Edna's house alongside a school cargo van. A police car with two uniformed police officers sitting inside was parked behind the van. One of the security guards opened the rear door of the van for Kai.

Kai climbed into the van. It was silent during the short ride to the school, the only sound coming from a security officer as he reported their progress to the school on a handheld radio.

Minutes later, the van turned into the school parking lot. A television reporter was standing on the sidewalk talking to an obviously agitated woman.

The passenger officer turned to face Kai. "There were a whole bunch of them here yesterday. It's a little quiet, today."

Kai nodded.

"You gonna keep playing football?"

It took Kai a moment to focus his attention on the guard. "What?"

"Are you still going to keep playing football?"

"If they let me."

"Good."

"Don't let what happens today get to you," the driver said. "You got a lot of people supporting you in the Heights. Mr. Meyers isn't as popular as he thinks he is."

They parked the van near the back of the school, and the security guards escorted Kai to the entrance of the building.

Several students stopped and stared at him, their eyes not unfriendly.

Kai ignored them, his eyes fixed dead ahead as he strode purposefully into the building. Inside, the chaos of students heading in all directions toward their respective classes dampened when they saw Kai.

The security guards left when he entered the Journalism classroom. The plan had been for them to escort him to and from school. During the day, the school administration believed Kai would be safe on campus. There was no way Thurman Adams was going to get on campus without being discovered.

The students stared at Kai as he entered the classroom and walked through the aisle toward his seat. He ignored them.

His eyes briefly met Patty's before he sat down, and he was surprised when he saw her emotional reaction. She had tears in her eyes.

Kai sat down.

Marcus Robinson got up from his desk.

"Good morning, Mr. Moore," Robinson said.

Kai nodded in response. He looked around the room. Nearly everyone had turned in their desks and were looking back at him. A few of the students stared at him as if he were a pariah. Others looked frightened.

"Shit," he muttered under his breath. He needed to do something about this before it got out of hand. He sighed and got up from his seat.

"You're not leaving, are you?" Robinson said.

"Can I say something to the class?"

"Please do."

He looked around at the students. "I think maybe some of you want me outta' here. If you want me to leave, that's what I'll do. I'll leave!" He paused for a moment and looked down at Patty.

She was staring up at him, tears streaming down her cheeks.

Kai looked back up at his classmates and paused for a moment before speaking again.

"But where do I go?" he continued. "Tell me that. Where do I go? I can't go back home! They broke into our house, killed my mother, and then someone burned it down. I can't even go back to Saint Ignatius. Some punk got into the school and tried to stick me with a knife. So, what in the hell do you want me to do?"

There was no response. Just stares, most of them now softened.

"So, what do you want me to do?" Kai repeated.

The only sound in the classroom was made by Marcus Robison as he sat heavily in his chair.

Kai bit his lip, determined not to be intimidated by the silence. "I'll tell you what I'm not going to do! I am not going to quit school! I'm not going to quit football! So, if you want me to quit, it's you that got the problem, cause I'm not goin' to leave this school until I graduate next June!"

Some of the classmates nodded their heads in affirmation; some had tears in their eyes; a few others looked doubtful. Patty reached out and touched his arm.

Kai sat down.

Verna Adams was washing out her coffee cup when she looked out the kitchen window and saw someone lying on the porch swing out back. She gasped for air when she realized who it was. It took her nearly five minutes before she collected herself and went outside.

She paused for a moment looking down at her son. "Boy, wake up. Whatchu doin' here? Cops are down the street, looking at this house."

Thurman shuddered, startled at suddenly being awakened. He looked up at his mother and then pushed himself up to a sitting position.

"Cops been lookin' for you, Thurman. You can't stay here."

Verna Adams watched him as he rubbed his eyes.

"Where have you been staying'?" she continued. "In the sewers? You smell like a swamp rat."

Thurman looked up at her. "I need your help. I need to hang out here for a couple of hours."

Angelo Rodriguez stood near the closed door to Ferrentini's office as Kai, looking serious, came out. He nodded to Angelo indicating that everything was okay.

"So, what happened?" Angelo asked.

"I don't think Ferrentini was happy about it, but I get to stay on the team."

Both boys were wearing the required dress for the weight room; white T-shirts trimmed in scarlet and scarlet shorts trimmed in white, one of the requirements laid out in Ferrentini's Rules Manual.

"That's good news," Angelo said.

Kai shrugged. "We'll see. Won't do much good if all I get to do is sit on my ass on the sideline."

The weight room was crowded. Buster Hollister sat nearby on a weight bench with a sly grin on his face, watching Red Meyers poke feebly at a punching bag.

"My sister can hit that thing as hard as you," Buster Hollister said.

"I know your sister," Red said. "That's a compliment."

Laughter broke out in the weight room but suddenly stopped when Kai and Angelo entered the room.

Red turned around and saw Kai approaching him.

Kai pointed to the punching bag.

"You using this, Meyers?"

Red showed off a smart-assed grin, knowing others were watching.

"So, Moore, what do we call you now? Kai, Ryan, or . . . duh killer?"

Kai balled up his fists and moved closer to Red.

"I'm getting tired of your shit, Meyers! You haven't pulled your weight on this football team since we played against Foothill. You can take the State record and shove it up your ass!"

The two boys glared at each other, eyeball-to-eyeball.

"You want to hit me, don't you Red?" Kai continued. "Come on, dragon breath! I'll give you the first shot!"

Someone called from across the weight room. "Watch out Red. They say he fought Golden Gloves!"

Red looked helplessly around the room for support.

Hollister got up from the bench and approached them, a rare look of concern on his face.

"Hey, lighten up guys."

Kai stepped toward the punching bag and hit it with a vicious blow.

The bag broke loose from its mooring and rocketed across the room. He then turned to face Red who had a look of terror on his face.

"I used to box, Meyers. Nobody and I mean nobody ever touched my face! And the reason was I let myself get so filled up with hate when I fought that I destroyed any punk that got in my way . . . just like that bag!"

The two of them were now so close that their noses were almost touching. "Now I don't hate you, Red. But I am getting awfully damn close!"

Kai spun around on his heels and stormed out of the weight room just as a startled Coach Prince walked in.

Prince paused for a moment, looking around at the shocked faces, and then said, "Okay. Listen up, everybody! Team meeting right now in the gym. On the double!"

The team sat silently in the bleachers. Kai, elbows on his knees, hands clasping his face, sat next to Angelo who was watching him. The coaching staff, except for Ferrentini, were standing near the door to the basketball locker rooms. A sloppily-dressed heavy-set kid who was named Hop and was one of the team managers stood apart from the coaches.

Ferrentini entered and took center stage with the authority of a drill instructor. He looked over the assembled team for a few moments, his eyes lighting on individual players for brief moments, making sure that they understood that what he had to say was directed to them.

He didn't look happy, and his voice was harsh and loud when he began speaking.

"Listen up, people! I've heard enough bullshit about Kai Moore in the last twenty-four hours to last me a lifetime!"

Kai looked up at the coach with a look of mild surprise.

Ferrentini then looked directly at Red Meyers as he continued.

"Contrary to what some people are saying up here in the Heights, Kai Moore is not a murderer. And anyone who tells you that is not only a damn fool but a damn liar as well!" He shifted his gaze to encompass the entire team. "Kai Moore has given this team one hundred and ten percent, and we have given him nothing but shit in return. That is going to turn around, right now, people. He's our teammate and *you* will support him."

Ferrentini paused for a moment, his eyes running over individual players. "We are the Jefferson Heights Red Raiders. We are the meanest badasses in the Heights! This is our turf! No one and I mean no one is going to badmouth Kai Moore on this campus and get away with it!"

He wiped his mouth with the back of his hand and turned away for a moment with his head down. It was silent in the gymnasium. When Ferrentini turned to face the team, his voice was much softer.

"Listen to me . . . listen to me as if our entire season depends on it . . . because it does. If you cannot accept what I say here today, then you better go home tonight and kneel down and pray to the Almighty God that He will grant you the wisdom to understand that what I've told you is the goddamn truth! And if by tomorrow morning you can't accept what I'm saying, then some changes are goin' to be made."

Ferrentini looked at his assistant coaches. "Where's Hop?"

Hop stepped forward. "Right here, coach!"

Ferrentini turned back to the team. "If you don't find it in your heart to support a teammate that needs your help, turn in your equipment to Hop. And I don't give a shit if you started every friggin' game this year!"

Ferrentini then spun on his heels and approached Coach Casey. "Take them up in the hills for a three-mile run, John. Make it as miserable as you can."

Coach Casey stepped forward. "Okay people, we're gonna start getting ready for Fremont by taking a little run. Let's go!"

The team got up slowly.

"Damn it, I said right now!" Casey yelled. "Get your ass outside right now! On the double!"

The team scrambled for the doors.

Later that night, Thurman Adams, carrying a long bag strapped over his back, left his mother's place by lofting himself over a fence into a neighbor's backyard. It was midnight, and the lights in the neighbor's house were out. Lucky for him, there were no dogs. He emerged onto the sidewalk in front of the house and looked up and down. There was no one about. He began walking toward Los Angeles Street.

He felt like a different person tonight. The air seemed cooler and fresher, and he smelled of his mother's soap. His mother had made him take a shower after she had cut his hair to a fine fuzz. He was now wearing his deceased father's clothes, a black silk shirt, two sizes too large for him, which made it perfect for concealing his revolver. He wore black denim jeans and an Oakland Raiders baseball cap. He had tried on the sunglasses his mother had given him — she had said they made him look like a movie star — but it was too dark to wear them, so they were in his pocket.

The rifle and ammo he had stolen were in a long cloth bag designed to carry a snowboard that his mother had bought at a sporting goods store. The bag also contained a pair of binoculars his mother had loaned him and two cans of chili.

Thurman couldn't afford to be stopped by the police, so he walked across lawns and stayed under the darkness of the trees. He looked both ways before crossing Los Angeles Street. The one thing he didn't need was running across some cops. Not that he had any reservations about shooting cops, but their buddies got pissed when you did that, and they were all over the place, and they had guns and cars with radios in them. Thurman didn't want to kick up a fuss when he had something important to do.

He was headed to a house two blocks away that belonged to his mother's friend. He would be staying in her backyard that night and would be gone the next morning before she even got out of bed.

Chapter Twenty-Two

The next day, Thurman Adams, keeping an eye out for the police, strode down the sidewalk in a rundown neighborhood covered with gang graffiti and strewn with trash. It was mid-morning and he needed to get all the way out to Crenshaw Avenue where he hoped to find what he needed in the parking lot of a supermarket where there were plenty of cars with people who knew how to drive them. Thurman was now wearing the sunglasses his mother had given him, and he was carrying the long bag that contained the rifle over his shoulder.

Crenshaw Avenue was two miles away. It was a long walk and Thurman began sweating. He didn't feel as fresh as he did the night before.

When he finally got to Crenshaw, he didn't need to walk the half mile south where the supermarket was located. He found what he needed at the curb next to a phone booth on a gas station parking lot.

A scarlet-colored Ford Excursion, its motor running, was parked at the curb. An elegant Black man in a tuxedo named Terry Lewis was on the telephone in the booth. Lewis was in his mid-thirties, movie star handsome with flecks of gray beginning to show in his curly hair.

Thurman walked up to him. "Hey man, is that your car?"

Lewis turned, the phone to his ear, and held up a finger, signaling Thurman to wait a moment. He turned his back.

Thurman drew his revolver from under his shirt and jabbed it into Terry Lewis' back.

Terry Lewis quickly turned, saw the gun, and dropped the telephone. He slowly raised his hands. "Don't shoot, man. Don't shoot! I'll give you my wallet."

Lewis began reaching for his pocket.

Thurman stuck the gun in his face, and Lewis' hands shot right back up.

"I said, is that your damn car?"

Lewis eagerly nodded.

"Get in the car!"

Lewis put his hands down. "If you want the car, take it. The keys are inside."

Thurman pointed the gun at Lewis' nose. "Are you deaf? Get in the damn car!"

Lewis nodded. He began walking toward the SUV, keeping his eye glued on the revolver in Thurman's hand. Lewis got into the driver's side of the vehicle. For a moment, it looked like he had a chance to draw his gun when Thurman dropped the bag he was carrying onto the back seat.

But Thurman never left his eyes off him. He slid into the passenger seat, keeping his revolver trained on Lewis.

An hour later, they were driving through a narrow pass heading toward Palmdale in the Antelope Valley, part of the great Mojave Desert.

Lewis threw an occasional nervous glance at the revolver in Thurman's hand and saw that Thurman's eyes were always on him. So was the gun.

"Why you dressed like that?" Thurman asked. "You goin' to a funeral or somethin'?"

Lewis sighed. "Look man, I was going to a wedding. My fiancée and my daughter . . . everybody's waiting for me at the church. They probably called the police already. Why don't you take my SUV and let me go?"

Thurman jabbed the gun into Lewis' ribcage.

Lewis winced. "Man, take it easy. I'm doing what you asked."

Thurman jabbed Lewis in the ribs again for emphasis. "Whass dat?"

"What?"

"That thing in your waist."

Lewis looked down. "That's a cummerbund. It's part of the tux. I'm getting married. I have a daughter. Take my car and let me go."

Thurman jammed the gun against Lewis' temple. "Don't move or I'll blow your head off!"

Lewis froze. He locked both hands on the steering wheel and kept driving.

Thurman reached over and pulled out a small semi-automatic pistol from the cummerbund and looked at it appreciatively.

"That's a nice piece, man. What you gonna' do with it, dude? Kill your bitch on your wedding day?"

The scarlet SUV nosed down a dirt road and stopped at the edge of a large salt flat surrounded by desert. It was hot and the heat across the flat created a shimmering image of a body of water in the distance.

Terry Lewis got out of the Excursion and looked for an escape route. Miles and miles of desert surrounded by mountains in the distance. There was nowhere he could hide.

Thurman pointed the gun at Lewis and directed him to the front of the car. Lewis did as he was told and leaned over the hood as if expecting a search. The heat coming up from the hood burned his hands, and he quickly withdrew them.

"What are you doin', man?" Thurman asked. "This ain't no bullshit T.V. show! Get in duh damn car!" He waved the gun in the direction of the passenger side.

Lewis looked at him in disbelief, but he got into the SUV.

Thurman slid in behind the wheel of the Excursion, warily watching Terry Lewis. He placed his revolver in a door pocket. He removed Lewis' semi-automatic from under his shirt, took off the safety, transferred it to his left hand, and pointed it at Lewis.

"I can shoot with either hand if you try to lay some shit on me. Do you unnerstand what I'm sayin'?"

"I can handle that," Lewis said. "What are we doing out here, man? . . . Waiting for the mothership to land?"

"Cut out the bullshit, man, and show me how to drive this piece of shit."

Lewis stared at Thurman for a long beat before answering. "You do know that they have schools for this sort of thing in the city?"

Thurman glared at him.

"Man, you really are one screwed-up dude, aren't you?"

A dark look of insanity crossed Thurman's face, confirming what Lewis thought.

The sun beat down on the body of Terry Lewis as he lay dead on the salt flat. There was a bloody bullet hole in the middle of his forehead. His jacket had been removed and his white shirt and black trousers were covered with a thin layer of fine chalk-colored dust. Two black vultures were a few feet away, but they were not looking at the body. They were looking at a dark object that lay on the ground next to a vehicle that was nearly 500 feet away.

A small bright flash and a small puff of smoke erupted from the dark object. A bullet splatted the desert floor near the body, and a rifle shot fractured the air less than a second later.

The vultures flew off.

Thurman stood near the hood of the Terry Lewis' Excursion and adjusted the telescopic sights of the rifle with a small screwdriver while muttering something to himself in an unrecognizable language. He didn't like shooting while lying on the ground. It made his dark clothing look as if someone had hit him with a bag of flour. For his second shot, he took a firing position using the hood of the SUV as a bench rest. He pulled the trigger and fired.

The vultures were now back at the body and looking around. A bullet struck the body and violently displaced it, scattering the vultures. The sound of the echoing shot arrived a scant second later.

Thurman Adams looked in the binoculars once more. He knew he hit the body, but he couldn't tell where he hit it. He aimed the rifle again and fired shot after shot after shot into the body in an uncontrollable rage.

Chapter Twenty-Three

Jefferson Heights versus Fremont at Home

Kai didn't know what to expect as he ran onto the football field with his teammates to face Fremont on Friday night. He felt tense throughout most of the day while at school because it seemed as if everybody who dared to look at him stared as if he were an alien creature that had just landed on the planet. It was bothersome, but not unbearable, so he went to each of his classes, tuning out the reactions of his classmates and trying to concentrate on what his teachers were saying in class.

The reaction of the crowd at the game that night seemed normal, but what wasn't normal was the presence of three television crews whose cameras were focused on him. So, when the game started, he kept his back to the sideline away from the cameras and concentrated on the game.

Sergeant Sid Conners stood at the top row of the bleachers next to a bored police officer named Larry Sawyer who was looking down on the street behind the stadium. The game had just started, and Jefferson Heights had the ball.

Using his binoculars, Conners looked for Kai Moore on the opposite side of the field. He found him standing on the sideline next to Angelo Rodriguez.

Kai looked relaxed and confident.

Conners then turned his attention to the field where Tyler Jefferson dropped back for a pass and unloaded the ball just as a Fremont player blindsided him in the ribs. The pass was intercepted, and Jefferson Heights went into pursuit as the runner raced up the sideline.

The fans cheered when the Fremont runner nearly had his head taken off by Martines, the Jefferson Heights tight end.

"Did you see that?" Officer Sawyer said to Conners.

"Hell of a tackle!" Conners replied.

"No. I mean *that!*"

Conners turned to look at him. The police officer wasn't talking about the tackle. He was looking down on the street behind the stadium.

"Didn't Lieutenant Lewis have a red Excursion like that one?" Sawyer asked Conners.

When Conners turned to see where Sawyer was pointing, he got a brief glimpse of a red Ford Excursion making a left turn on a road that led up into the Heights.

That morning, Lieutenant Terry Lewis didn't show up for his wedding. When his best man went to his apartment to find out what happened to him, Lewis wasn't there, and neither was his Excursion. He had disappeared.

A missing person report was filed, and an emergency broadcast was made on all law enforcement radio frequencies to be on the lookout for his SUV and to contact the LAPD if the Excursion was found.

Conners rushed down from the stands followed by Sawyer.

As the two of them left the stadium parking lot in a marked police car a few moments later, Tyler Jefferson was being escorted off the field by the team doctor, and Angelo Rodriguez was warming up on the sideline.

Up in the Heights, the scarlet Ford Excursion that belonged to Lieutenant Terry Lewis was parked in a cul de sec, its front end facing the exit. A residence was located at the end of the cul de sac with its landscape lighting on and interior lights off. Other residences lined the street on the hillside, but the side of the street that faced the high school had no houses. The Excursion was parked at the curb next to the drop-off.

Thurman braced his rifle across the hood of the SUV and aimed it downhill towards the stadium. He had a problem adjusting the gun on the hot hood, and then another problem trying to find his target. Three hundred yards was a long distance away, and Thurman couldn't distinguish the faces of the football team and tell if they were white or black. He began looking for a white jersey with the number 27 on it. There was no player with that number on the field, so he began scanning the sideline.

He found one.

A player wearing number 27 with his helmet on was standing apart from his teammates on the sideline.

Thurman grunted. "You goin' down tonight, scrub."

He held the rifle steady and pulled the trigger.

A small patch of grass on the field in front of Kai was blasted into a puff of green dust.

No one heard the shot above the noise in the stadium.

Kai, sensing that something unusual had just happened, blinked his eyes. He felt some movement in the air, a puff of wind, nothing more. He turned his attention back to the field where Angelo Rodriguez was in the huddle.

A police car, its headlights out, pulled into the cul de sac where Thurman was trying to get another shot off.

Thurman looked up.

The car stopped and its headlights came on, momentarily blinding Thurman who shielded his eyes.

Seconds later, blinking emergency lights came on and lit up the street.

Conners jumped out of the passenger side of the car, and Officer Sawyer emerged from the driver's side. They drew their weapons and aimed Thurman.

"Thurman Adams, it's the police!" Conners yelled into the car's p.a. system. "Drop that gun and put up your hands!"

Thurman raised the rifle and fired a wild shot at Conners. The bullet shattered the police car's emergency lights, exploding shards of glass and plastic all over the officers. Thurman threw the rifle over the drop-off and jumped into the Excursion. Jamming the accelerator to the floor, he launched the Excursion, its wheels squealing, toward the exit of the cul de sac.

The big SUV narrowly missed Sawyer who jumped back into the police car to avoid being hit.

Conners whirled and fired three shots at the Excursion as it disappeared around a sharp left-hand turn and onto a street that headed onto a steep grade downhill. He jumped back into the police car, and Sawyer made a U-turn and took off after the SUV.

Seconds later, the police car roared out of the cul de sac at high speed with its emergency lights and siren on.

Conners yelled into the mike. "David 18 is in pursuit of a red Ford Excursion in Jefferson Heights."

Thurman who had only learned to drive that afternoon turned the Excursion through a sweeping downhill turn. The tires squealed as he held onto the steering wheel for dear life. The road then cut sharply to the right, and Thurman hit the brakes while trying to steer the SUV into the curve. Its back end slid out toward a Mercedes sedan parked on the other side of the street. A look of sheer terror crossed Thurman's face as the SUV sideswiped the sedan, bounced off, and miraculously continued down the street.

Seconds later, the police car slid through the corner in a cloud of dust and smoke. Conners was thrown violently sideways into his partner as they made the turn at high speed. He struggled to get his seat belt on.

Up ahead, the Excursion began passing several streets with drainage channels on either side of the intersection. They were not deep, but deep enough that the SUV bottomed out and threw off sparks as it bounced violently over them.

Meanwhile, Conners had lost his mike. He looked for it and found it rolling on the floor. He picked it up and yelled into it.

"David 18 in pursuit of a homicide suspect in a red Ford Excursion northbound on Shelby Road in Jefferson Heights! Shots fired! We need a chopper out here right now!"

The police car hit a drainage channel and was launched airborne. A trail of sparks erupted from the rear of the car as it bottomed out on the road, lighting up the interior.

Conners keyed his mike. "David 18! Did you roger that?"

He looked at the mike and then the radio. The light was out. Conners turned to the officer driving the car.

"We lost our radio! Don't lose this guy! Whatever you do, don't lose him!"

A minute later, the Excursion roared down the street behind the stadium bleachers at 100 miles an hour. The police car arrived three seconds later, its siren screaming. The spectators on the top rows of the bleachers turned to watch the police car go by.

Thurman approached the Pomona freeway underpass at high speed. A sign pointed left toward the Interstate. He jammed on the brakes and locked them up as he ineptly tried to turn the car to the left.

The Excursion slid through the intersection, spinning 180 degrees before it stopped. Thurman looked up and saw the police car racing towards him. He gunned the engine and launched the SUV toward the approaching police car.

The police car didn't slow down. It couldn't. Its brakes were gone.

Thurman violently wrenched the steering wheel to the right.

Inside the police car, Conners and Sawyer had twin expressions of pure terror on their faces.

"Brace yourself!" the police officer yelled to Conners. "My brakes are gone!"

The police car veered sharply right to avoid the collision with the SUV. It hit the curb, blowing both tires.

The impact launched the car airborne. It threaded a needle between a streetlamp and a utility pole before landing on the sidewalk and finally rolling to a stop on flattened tires.

Conners jumped out of the police car and ran up to the entrance to the Interstate. He saw the SUV accelerating up the ramp and then disappear onto the freeway. He ripped off his hat and threw it to the ground.

"Well, kiss my big fat ass! The sonovabitch learned how to drive."

Chapter Twenty-Four

It was late in the game with less than five minutes left to play and Fremont leading 21 to 20. Tyler Jefferson was back in the game. He casually walked up to the center, and after looking over the defensive formation, he glanced back at Red Meyers.

Red nodded in return.

Tyler felt confident they would win the game. They were on Fremont's thirty-one-yard line and in a position to score a field goal if necessary.

Several Fremont players were now excitedly pointing to Jefferson Height's left side. Their captain, the middle linebacker yelled, "Strong right, strong right!"

Tyler looked at the play clock. Fremont had guessed where the play was going to be run. It was too late to change it. Tyler took the snap and pitched the ball to Red.

He didn't get far.

A defensive tackle broke through the line and hit Red as he was trying to gain control of the ball. He fumbled and went down hard.

A Fremont linebacker recovered the football and cheers erupted from the small crowd on their side of the field.

There was a stunned silence in the Jefferson Heights stands. It looked as if Fremont had the chance to win the game.

Three minutes later, Fremont wasn't able to take advantage of the fumble and their punt team was setting up on their thirty-six-yard line.

Kai Moore was bouncing on his toes and waiting for the punt on the Jefferson Heights forty.

A movement on the Fremont sideline caught his attention. He froze when he saw what was happening. A Fremont player had slipped onto the field from the bench and took a wide receiver position near the sideline.

No one was covering him!

Kai's eyes shifted to the Fremont offensive line. Two of the Fremont players were set back in their stances. Fremont was not going to kick the ball. They were setting up for a pass.

Kai shouted a warning to his teammates. "Wide out left! Wide out left!"

Unfortunately, the noise from the fans drowned him out.

He broke from his position and ran across the field toward the Fremont wide receiver.

On the sideline, Ferrentini exploded. "What in the hell is he doing out there?"

Kai yelled as he ran towards the receiver who snuck onto the field. "Pass! . . . pass! . . . pass! . . . pass!"

The ball was snapped. The punter took the snap and threw a pass to the wide receiver who was now streaking downfield.

The receiver turned, looking for the ball.

Kaa fixed his eyes on the ball as he bore down on the receiver. He cut in front of him and leaped in the air, catching the ball like a falcon nailing a small bird in flight. He hit the ground in full stride and raced untouched to the goal line.

There was pandemonium in the Jefferson Heights stands.

On the sideline, Ferrentini imitated a crapshooter rolling dice.

Kai was met coming out of the end zone by his teammates, who pounded him on the back. The next thing they heard was a chilling announcement on the stadium public address system.

"There's a flag on the play."

The celebration ceased, and the team captains anxiously gathered around the referee.

Seconds later, the Jefferson Heights captain reacted in jubilation as the referee moved away from the players.

The referee signaled by rolling his hands in front of him. "Illegal procedure on the kicking team. The penalty is declined. The touchdown stands."

Kai Moore had scored the winning touchdown.

Kai, wearing football breeches and a tee-shirt, was alone in the weight room and working up a sweat on a punching bag. He felt the need to get away from his teammates who had suffocated him in their enthusiasm for what he had done.

He could hear the muffled voices of the jubilant team in the locker even though the door was closed. The noise increased as the door opened, but Kai didn't turn to see who entered. He continued hitting the bag until he heard a recognizable voice behind him.

"Hey, Kai Moore!"

Kai turned and saw Sid Conners.

The burly detective was in shirtsleeves. He was not wearing a gun.

"I heard you had a nice game. The winning touchdown! Congratulations!"

Kai smiled. "Hey, Sergeant Conners. What's up?"

Conners pointed to the bag. "Didn't you get enough exercise tonight?"

"Not as much as I did when I played at Saint Ignatius. I hardly broke a sweat."

There was silence for a beat as Kai watched Conners intently.

"Okay, Sergeant Conners, what's goin' on?"

Conners sighed. "Adams was up here tonight looking for you."

"Did you get him?"

"He was driving a red SUV. He got away."

"How did he do that? You, you . . . you said he couldn't drive!"

"He can't drive. I mean he couldn't drive. But he stole an SUV and somehow learnt how to drive the damn thing!"

Kai sat down dejectedly on a weight bench.

"Father Mike's scared, Kai. He wants to pull you out of school, but Edna won't let him. She's a tough old bird."

Kai got up and stared at the punching bag.

"I finally got a chance to play some football out here, Sergeant Conners," he said in a whisper.

Conners reached in his pocket and held up two shell casings in a plastic bag.

"These came from a rifle that Thurman ditched. He popped one of these at us, and I'm pretty damn sure he popped one at you."

Kai paused for a moment, felt anger rising, and then turned away.

He hit the punching bag as hard as he could.

Conners flinched.

"Damn! You still got it, boy!" Conners said. "We've got to get you back in the ring."

Boxing was the last thing on Kai's mind. He was thinking about Thurman Adams and what to do about him.

"I'll be watching your back, boy," Conners continued. "We'll have your house covered around the clock." He paused for a moment. "Did you know that Edna McKay keeps a revolver in the house?"

Kai nodded.

Conners sighed and then looked at the floor.

"Let me tell you something else. We have a detective lieutenant by the name of Terry Lewis who has gone missing. He had a red SUV like the one that Adams was driving tonight. We can't find him or his SUV. We're not playing a game here with some minor league cowboy, Kai. You need to be careful every damn minute of the day."

Maybe, Kai thought, he finally needed to do something about Thurman Adams. He had an idea that began formulating in the back of his mind.

After Conners left, Kai went back to the locker room and asked Angelo Rodriguez if he had a car.

Chapter Twenty-Five

Conners had promised Kai that he would have round-the-clock protection, yet when Kai left the house that morning on the long walk up to the high school, he saw no evidence of any police officers.

That was fine by him.

A half hour after Kai had liberated Edna's gun from her bedroom, he was waiting on the sidewalk in front of the high school. He had left a note at the house, telling Edna he had gone to the high school to work out.

He was wearing a bulky blue windbreaker that concealed the gun in his waistband.

Minutes later, Angelo pulled up to the curb in a blue Miata convertible with the top down.

Kai got into the Miata.

Angelo looked at the jacket Kai was wearing. "Are you afraid of catching a cold or something?"

"Angelo, I need a favor. I need to borrow your car."

Angelo hesitated for a moment before answering. "Can you drive?"

"Yes."

"Do you have a license?"

Kai shook his head.

"Where do you want to go?" Angelo asked, a big smile on his face.

"Downtown. A place called Mickie's Fight Club."

"I'll drive you there."

"I might be there all day. Besides, it's gonna be dangerous."

"This involves that guy that's after you?"

Kai nodded.

"I'll drive you there."

"Angelo, you don't want to go down there."

Angelo smiled, put the car in gear, and drove away from the curb.

The street where Kai used to live with his mother in Echo Park was quiet. Angelo drove his car slowly up the street.

Kai turned in his seat when he spotted the vacant lot where the house had been. He held up his hand, signaling Angelo to stop the car, and then pointed to the curb.

After Angelo parked the car, he followed Kai's gaze to a weed-infested lot. All that remained of the house was the foundation which was now pockmarked with weeds.

"That was where your house was?" Angelo asked. The smile that was always on his face was no longer there.

Kai nodded, not saying anything.

A half hour later, Angelo parked his car so that it was partially hidden at the back of the parking lot next to Mickie's Fight Club.

The side entrance of Mickie's was in view.

"What are we waiting for?" Angelo asked.

"I didn't ask you to come along."

Angelo, astonished, looked at him. "You don't have to be so rude about it. You're lookin' for that guy that killed your mother, aren't you?"

Kai didn't say anything in response.

Angelo shifted in his seat. "Kai, this is dangerous."

"I already told you that, Angelo. You agreed to bring me here, so quit whining."

Angelo shrugged, said nothing.

Two hours later, Angelo bored, pulled a book out of the glovebox, and began reading. It was *Great Expectations* by Dickens.

A bum wandered across the parking lot and stopped in front of the Miata. He stared at Kai who stared back. The bum gave him a finger and shuffled off.

"I'm sorry," Kai said.

"What?" Angelo said, distracted.

"I'm sorry . . . for what I said . . . for getting you involved in this."

"Forget it," Angelo said as he shifted in his seat. "Are you hungry?"

"No."

"I am."

"There's a good hamburger stand one block south on Hill Street."

"I'm not leaving you here alone," Angelo said as he watched the bum rifling through a dumpster.

Later still, the sun was setting. Angelo was napping.

Kai was still alert. He sat up when he saw Sergeant Sid Conners hurriedly emerge from the gym. Kai tried to sink down in his seat to hide but couldn't. Fortunately, Conners never looked in their direction. He got into a car and drove off.

It was getting dark. The Miata was hidden in the shadows at the back of the lot. A familiar figure walked across the lot from the street and entered the gym through the side door. It wasn't Thurman Adams, but it was someone who might know where he was.

Kai opened the car door and Angelo jumped awake.

"What's going on?"

"Stay here. I'll be right back."

Kai entered the gym from the side door and walked down a dimly lit hallway. He peered around a corner into the main room of the gym. A few wannabe fighters were working the bags. In the ring were two fighters really going at each other under the supervision of their trainer, a hulking Black man whose bald head shined like a beacon under the fluorescent lights.

A few minutes later, Kai caught sudden movement at the rear of the gym. Lamont Jamison had just entered the gym from a hallway.

Lamont saw Kai and froze. He turned and beat a hasty retreat.

Kai went after him, not caring if anyone in the gym had spotted him.

The gym manager, who everyone called Bones, was seated at the desk in his glass-walled office. He looked up and saw Kai moving quickly across the gym floor. He picked up the telephone with some urgency.

The trainer in the ring noticed his two fighters had stopped sparring and were staring at someone behind him. He turned and saw Kai.

The gym became so quiet that you could hear a mouse burp.

Kai stopped when he became aware all had gone quiet. He turned to find that everyone in the gym was looking at him.

"Does anyone know where I can find Thurman Adams?" Kai asked.

"He don't come here no more," the big trainer said. "*You* need to git."

"I didn't ask if he came here no more. I asked if anybody knows where I can find him."

No one answered.

Kai looked at each of the faces in the gym one by one and then said, "If anybody here knows where he is, tell him I'll be back later tonight."

He left the gym.

It was now dark, and Angelo had put his book away. He saw Kai come out of the gym and started the car.

Kai got into the Miata and looked at Angelo. "Where are you goin'? I'm not done."

Angelo shut off the ignition, looked at his watch, and sighed.

"You can leave if you want," Kai said. "I can find a way to get home. I have enough money for a taxi."

"If you're staying, I'm staying," Angelo said.

Later, Kai was hunched down in his seat, his eyes half-closed. Angelo had nodded off.

A tall figure emerged from the sidewalk and walked toward the side entrance of Mickie's gym. He stepped into the light under the entrance and opened the door.

Kai sat up when he saw the man. He looked like Thurman Adams, but he wasn't sure. He shook Angelo awake.

"What's going on?" Angelo asked.

Kai zipped open his jacket and pulled out Edna's gun.

"Holy shit, Kai! What are you doin'?"

"If I don't come back in five minutes, get outta here and don't come back."

Kai stepped out of the car and stopped when he heard a police siren wailing in the distance. Satisfied that the sound seemed to be going away, he continued across the lot toward Mickie's Fight Club.

At the rear of the lot, Thurman Adams emerged from the alley behind Mickie's carrying a gun. He raised the gun and aimed it at Kai.

A police car roared into the lot from the street and illuminated Kai in its headlights. It screeched to a stop.

Thurman heard car doors open and then a loudspeaker opened up from the police car. "DROP THAT GUN,AND PUT UP YOUR HANDS!"

He realized they weren't talking to him, but to the boy he had known as Ryan Moore. For just a moment, Thurman entertained the idea of shooting the boy in the back but then realized if he did that, he would piss off the police and they would start shooting at him.

Thurman muttered to himself and darted back into the alley under the cover of darkness.

Chapter Twenty-Six

Kai was made to forcefully lie down on the dirty parking lot by a big police officer name Garza who began roughly handcuffing him. Kai turned his head to see what had happened to Angelo. The Miata was still parked at the back of the lot, but he couldn't see if Angelo was in it.

Garza grabbed Kai by the collar, pulled him to his feet, and led him roughly to the squad car. His partner was a stunning female officer named Partridge who looked as if she belonged in a recruiting poster aimed at enticing models to join LAPD.

Once Garza had seated Kai in the back seat of the police car, he examined the revolver he took from him.

"What were you going to do with this gun, buddy?"

Kai didn't answer.

Garza gave the revolver to Partridge and then leaned into the police car.

"How old are you?" Garza asked.

"Do you know Sergeant Sid Conners?" Kai asked, hopefully.

"Answer my question. How old are you?"

"Seventeen . . ."

"Like hell you are!" Garza said. "And to answer your question, in my humble opinion, Sid Conners is a first-class asshole. I never liked him." Garza stared at him for a moment, looking him up and down. "You've been in the joint, haven't you? All buffed out like that?"

"What are you talking about? I'm seventeen. I've never been arrested. . . ."Look, if you could . . ."

Garza didn't let him finish. "Do you have i.d.?"

"No."

"Then you go in the adult lock-up."

Garza stood up and walked a few steps away from the car taking his partner with him. They began talking in a low tone of voice.

Kai tried to hear what they were saying but couldn't hear anything. He wondered if all police officers were as strange as Garza. Even the gun in his holster was different than what other police officers carried. It was a revolver, not a semi-automatic, and it was long, at least seven or eight inches long.

The next thing Kai heard was something that disturbed him even more. The female officer was giggling.

What is so damn funny about arresting someone? Kai thought.

En route to the police station, Garza was behind the wheel of the police car while Partridge sat next to Kai in the back seat. She leaned closer to him, apparently wanting to tell him something. Her perfume smelled of fresh strawberries, and Kai realized he hadn't eaten anything since breakfast.

"You made him mad," the female officer said in a whisper. She pointed at Garza. "Do you know who he is?"

Kai shrugged, resigned to his fate. Before the night was over, he was going to be in Juvenile Hall.

"They call him Kneecap," Partridge continued. "The only thing that saved your butt was when you dropped that gun so quickly. You'd have been the eighth notch on his gun."

Kai stared directly ahead as the police car pulled into the parking lot behind Police Headquarters.

Kai had been in a police station before, so he knew he was in a detective squad room which was only occupied by two detectives who were working at their desks and the two officers who had arrested him. Partridge was at a long table writing a report while Garza wandered aimlessly around the squad room.

When Garza glanced at him, Kai called out to him. "Could you let Sergeant Conners know that I want to talk to him?"

"Pretty please?" Garza said in a mincing voice that was irritating as all hell.

Kai bit his lip and then said, "Please, sir."

"No!"

After Partridge finished the report, Kai was led by Garza down a hallway toward the back of Police Headquarters and into the nightmarish hell of the city jail. They passed a holding cell filled with several dozen sleeping drunks lying on a cement floor. A man was down on his knees puking into a commode. They passed a smaller cell that held a man dressed in women's clothes. He was curled up in a corner weeping. Another cell had a man with a gaping hole where his left eye had been. He was furiously shaking the steel bars as he watched Garza lead Kai down the hallway.

Kai shuddered.

"Nice place, huh?" Garza said. "They say you get use to the smell . . . and the screaming at night."

They arrived at the end of the hallway where Garza placed Kai in an empty cell.

Once Kai was inside, he sat down on a metal bench.

Garza slammed the door shut and left.

Depressed, Kai laid down on the bench and began to think of his predicament. He didn't know much about police procedures, but he knew he was entitled to a phone call. One had not been offered to him. Maybe, he should have asked. He dozed off, thinking about how unreal everything seemed. An hour later, he fell into a troubled sleep on the hard bench.

Later, a nightmarish scream echoed throughout the jail and woke him up.

Kai sat up and listened for a beat. Just as he was about to lie down again, he heard someone whispering. He got up and went to the cell door. Two men were talking in the cell next to his.

"They never caught me," someone said in a hoarse voice. "Every time I eat lettuce, I think of her."

"Why lettuce?"

"I took her to where I work and dumped her in a vat filled with chicken guts. They grind them up and use them for fertilizer. The batch she was in was sent to a farm where they grow lettuce."

The two men laughed hysterically, one so violently that he began coughing.

Kai went back to the metal bench, a look of horror on his face. He heard another voice yell out, "Shut up and go to sleep!"

The two men in the cell next to Kai's laughed even harder. Kai laid down and covered his ears with his hands.

Chapter Twenty-Seven

Sunlight streamed through a barred window when Kai woke up. He turned over, stiff and sore from sleeping on the metal bench without a pillow. He opened his eyes when he realized that someone was in the cell.

Sid Conners sat on a metal stool watching him. Garza who was now wearing a blue T-shirt and jeans leaned against the cell door. He was smiling in sort of a sickening way.

"So, what do you think?" Conners asked. "You like it here?"

Kai rolled to a sitting position. "Sid!"

"That's Sergeant Conners to you, boy." He held up Edna McKay's gun. "Do you think Edna knows you took this?"

"No, sir."

"I'm not even going to ask what you intended to do with this . . . what with Officer Garza being here and all. Good thing you dropped this gun last night because Garza would have put a bullet in your kneecap. And then no more football for you, boy."

"Sergeant Conners, I'm sorry. I-I-"

"Want another chance? Was that what you were going to say, boy?"

"Yes, sir."

"You don't like it here?"

"No, sir."

Conners got up. "I thought you wanted to play football."

"Yes, sir. I do."

"Then what in hell were you thinkin'of . . . stealin' a gun from Mrs. McKay?"

"I didn't steal her gun."

"You just borrowed it, eh?"

"Yes, sir."

"Bullshit! If you don't know what stealin' is by now, boy, there's no hope for you."

Conners stomped out of the cell. He slammed the cell door shut and left with Garza.

Later, Kai tried to look out the barred window by bouncing up and down on his toes, but he did not have the height. He sat on his bunk and stared at the floor.

"Kai."

He looked up.

Conners was opening the cell door.

"Let's make a deal. You play football . . . and you let me take care of Thurman Adams. Agreed?"

Kai stared at him for a moment before understanding what Conners had said.

"Agreed."

"Okay. Let's go."

Kai sat alongside Conners as he drove a plainclothes car on the freeway toward Jefferson Heights. Conners glanced at Kai.

"You're lucky that Mrs. McKay has got a heart. She agreed to take you back. Otherwise, you'd be on your way to Juvenile Hall now."

"Sid, I'm sorry."

"Thank God it's Sunday and Father McKay won't be there. When I talked to him, he surprised the hell out of me with his vocabulary, him being a priest and all. He probably needs to go back to the seminary for re-education."

Edna, dressed for church, stood in the middle of her living room, her arms folded. "I trusted you, Kai. How could you do this?"

"I'm sorry, Mrs. McKay."

Sid Conners handed Edna the gun and the bullets. Edna stared at it for a moment and then looked up at Kai. "What were you goin' to do with this gun?"

"You don't want to be asking him that in front of me," Conners said.

Edna put the gun in her purse. "I guess I'll have to keep this locked up." She looked at Kai. "Well, I'm not going to let you ruin my day. I'm going to church. You stay in your room until dinnertime. Can I trust you not to steal anything else from me?"

"Yes ma'am."

"Call me Edna," she said as she walked out the door.

Kai watched her leave.

"Well, that wasn't too bad," he said.

"Wait until Father McKay gets here," Conners said. "He was hopping mad this morning."

When Father Mike finally arrived, there was no lecture. He seemed more interested in the dinner he was eating than what had happened last night. Even though he was dressed casually, wearing a black sweater and jeans, he still looked like a priest.

After taking a few bites of dinner at the small table in the kitchen that Edna preferred over the massive table in the dining room, Kai set his fork down and said to Father Mike, "When are we going to talk about what happened last night?"

Father Mike chewed his food for a while, and Kai was sure that the priest had not heard what he asked.

Finally, the priest put his fork down and burst out laughing. "I heard you had an extraordinary night. Sid told me all about it."

Kai decided not to push it. The priest was in a good mood, and he wondered what Conners had told him that had that effect on him.

After dinner was finished and Edna was making coffee, Kai pushed away from the table and stood up.

"Mrs. McKay, may I use the telephone?"

"May I ask why?" Edna asked.

"I need to call Angelo."

"Did he take you down there . . . to that awful place?"

"I need to find out if he's okay."

Angelo brushed over Kai's apology and said, "There's something I need to tell you about what happened last night. You better thank God those cops got there when they did. They saved your butt."

"Yeah, they saved my butt all right. They kept me locked up overnight, and . . ."

Angelo cut him off. "Kai, there was a guy down there coming after you with a gun."

"What are you talking about?"

"When you were walking across the lot, there was a crazy-looking dude that came out of the alley. He was looking at you. He had a gun."

"Was he wearing an Afro?"

"No, his hair was short. He was almost bald."

"I didn't see him. What happened to him?"

"He backed away when he saw that police car."

Kai pondered this information before responding.

Thurman Adams always wore an Afro. Why the sudden change?

"I owe you one, Angelo," Kai finally said. "Thanks."

"That's not all," Angelo said. "I think the whole thing was a set-up."

"What do you mean?" Kai asked.

"The officers that arrested you. Once they had you in the car, they went around to the back and were laughing so hard that their faces turned red. When they went to get in the car, they were all serious again."

After Angelo hung up, Kai thought about what he had said. He remembered thinking about how there was something funny about the way he was processed. They never searched him when they took him back to the jail. They never offered him a phone call, even though he was entitled to one. They never even read him his Constitutional rights.

Weren't they supposed to do that?

He thought back to when he entered the gym, about the look of surprise that Bones had on his face when he spotted Kai. The gym manager was a friend of Sergeant Conners. He probably would have called Sergeant Conners rather than 911 if there was trouble in the gym.

Kai suddenly noticed Edna and Father Mike were watching him.

"Is anything wrong," Edna asked.

"Thurman Adams," Kai said distractedly. "He outsmarted me last night. He's not goin' to give up."

Chapter Twenty-Eight

Jefferson Heights versus Marshall at Home

With the Jefferson Heights Red Raiders tied with the Marshall Tigers 7 to 7 at the beginning of the second quarter, a harried Tyler Jefferson glanced at Ferrentini as he returned to the huddle. He tried not to show the sharp pain in his ribs after he had just been drilled into the turf by nearly half of the Marshall defense. He saw Ferrentini's signal, left hand three fingers, right hand one finger, and then looked at the armband on his wrist containing a list of plays.

He entered the huddle and made a point of looking at each member of the line.

"Did you guys ever hear of a concept in football called blocking?"

No one answered.

Strangely enough, Tyler felt satisfied. The offensive line had not given up. There was a look of determination in their glazed eyes. Marshall had one hell of a defense, but Tyler believed his offensive line would eventually wear them down.

"Okay, listen up," Tyler said. "Forty-four pass, double-wide right on set."

"That's a pass play, Tyler," Red Meyers said. "He didn't call a pass."

"The coach signed a Forty-four pass."

"He signaled Thirty-four, option right!"

Tyler looked at the chart on his armband and then at Red. He shook his head, trying to throw off a budding headache before looking back at Red.

"You better not be doing this again, Red." Tyler looked at the sideline hoping that Ferrentini would send the signal again.

Ferrentini was furiously winding his arm, signifying hurry-up.

Tyler made the call, and the team broke out of the huddle. Before Tyler took his position behind the center, he glanced at Ferrentini, who was shaking his head. It was at that moment Tyler realized the coach wasn't happy about the way the team was lining up, and that Red had lied about the call.

It was too late to do anything about it now.

He took the snap, and spun to the left, looking for Red Meyers. Someone tackled him from behind just as he pitched the ball to Red. When he looked up from the ground, he saw that Red had only made one yard before he was cut down by the defense. Tyler swore under his breath.

As he got up, he heard Ferrentini calling him. Ferrentini's clipboard was on the ground, which was a bad sign. He had seen Ferrentini throw his clipboard on the ground before when he didn't like what he saw on the field.

Tyler trotted wearily to the hash marks.

"Where in hell was my pass?" Ferrentini yelled.

"Red said you called a Thirty-four option right."

"Dammit, listen to me boy! Forty-four pass, double-wide right!"

Tyler was furious when he returned to the huddle. He took his anger out on Red Meyers.

"You dick! You lied again and I took the heat for it."

"Kiss my ass!"

Tyler always had doubts about Red as a team player, but what happened next made that point quite clear. He took the snap, dropped smartly back for a pass, and was stunned when he saw Red let a blitzing linebacker slip by. Tyler tried to scramble, but before he could get his momentum going, the linebacker smashed into his side and slammed him into the ground.

The referee signaled a timeout as Tyler writhed in pain.

Ferrentini, on the sideline, turned to Coach Prince. "Get the punting team in, Wally."

"Meyers let that guy break through on purpose," Prince said.

Ferrentini nodded in agreement as he watched Tyler being escorted off the field by the team doctor. He decided to watch the punt return by Marshall before checking on Tyler.

Marshall picked up fifteen yards on the punt return.

Ferrentini swore under his breath and went to find Tyler.

Tyler was sitting on the bench with his helmet off, his head down over his knees.

"How is he?" Ferrentini asked the doctor.

"Contusion to the ribs. Nothing broken, I think. He'll need to sit this one out."

Tyler looked up at Ferrentini, anguish in his eyes. "I can play coach . . . as soon as I get my breath back."

His face was flushed. He was in no condition to play against a team as good as Marshall.

Ferrentini bent over Tyler and whispered in his ear. "We'll get you back in for the second half." He returned to the sideline in time to see the Marshall quarterback run for ten yards before he slipped and fell while making a cut.

Marshall was on the move, and Ferrentini felt as if the game was slipping away from him. He turned to Coach Prince.

"Where's Rodriguez?"

Prince pointed down the line. Angelo was warming up behind the bench, throwing passes to Paul Bishop.

When Ferrentini returned to the sideline, he found Red Meyers waiting for him.

"Coach, I need to talk to you."

"You're blocking my view, Meyers. Get your ass to the bench and sit down!"

"Coach, it wasn't my fault. I didn't see that guy!"

"Get your ass on the bench right now!"

Red walked away.

Ferrentini turned back to the field in time to see an unguarded Marshall wide receiver racing past the bench.

The Marshall quarterback threw a bomb. The receiver caught the ball and scored a touchdown. The scoreboard changed showing Marshall up by 6.

The fans on the Marshall side of the field cheered wildly, seeing a championship in their future.

On the sideline, Ferrentini surveyed his somber team. The confidence they had displayed earlier in the game was gone. He saw Kai Moore standing by himself, looking out onto the field with his arms crossed. Ferrentini called his name and waved him over.

"Moore, are you ready to play?"

"Yes, sir!"

"Listen up. Marshall got a silly idea in their head that they can beat us. I think maybe you and Rodriguez can bust their bubble. Do you agree?"

Kai smiled. "Yes, sir."

The Marshall kicker booted a long one, sending the ball into the end zone. The first play that Ferrentini called was a pass play. Angelo Rodriguez dropped back, looking for his receivers. The same linebacker that had put Tyler out of the game had Angelo in his sights when Kai laid a block into him so hard it sent him tumbling to the ground without a helmet.

The pass was caught by Martines, the tight end, for a five-yard gain.

There was a short time out as the linebacker finally got up from the ground and limped off the field with two medical attendants holding him up by the arms.

On the next play, Angelo fired a pass to Bishop who caught it on a post pattern and picked up fifteen yards before he was brought down.

The next play was another pass, this time to Kai who shot through a gap in the line and spun around to catch a bullet from Angelo. He sidestepped the middle linebacker and gained another eleven yards before he was brought down.

There was a palpable shift in momentum as the Red Raiders had in three plays penetrated Marshall territory. It was the Tigers' turn to have worried looks on their faces.

The next play was one that Kai liked. It was an option play with the offensive line sliding left to lead the blocking. Angelo pitched the ball to Kai who slipped through a gap and beat the defensive unit to the goal line.

Kai had several advantages as a player. He was fast and could outrun nearly every defensive player in the league. He was strong and would not go down easily when hit, often pushing back a gang of tacklers for another five yards before going down and even on occasion breaking free. He showed that ability near the end of the second half when on the Marshall nine-yard line, Angelo dropped back to pass but handed off to Kai who burst through a sliver of a hole. He dodged a linebacker and was hit at the two-yard line by two Tiger defenders. Kai, his feet churning the ground, drove them back into the end zone for a touchdown.

But Kai had another advantage, an advantage that helped against a team with strong defenders. He was agile.

Once Kai had the ball in his hands, he could sharply cut right or left and sidestepped a defensive player before he knew what was happening.

By the end of the game, Kai had scored four touchdowns. By the end of the game. Angelo had the biggest smile that Kai had ever seen.

Tyler Jefferson never came back into the game, and Angelo had completed twelve of sixteen passes, including a touchdown pass for sixty-two yards to wide receiver Phil Marley.

The Red Raiders offense under Angelo Rodriguez energized the defensive unit who kept the vaunted Tigers out of the endzone, forcing them to settle for two field goals.

Jefferson Heights beat Marshall 42 to 20.

Thurman Adams and several men were drinking beer and playing pool in the dingy poolroom of a rundown bar on East Fifth Street in downtown Los Angeles. A small television tucked in a forgotten corner showed the end of the Jefferson Heights/Marshall game with an enthusiastic broadcaster nearly shouting as he recapped the game.

"And as Jefferson Heights celebrates a stunning victory over Marshall in the suburbs, we have just received news that Saint Ignatius has defeated Westwood, forty-five to fourteen. So next week we have a rematch of last year's battle between the Jefferson Heights Red Raiders and the Saint Ignatius Warriors for the Mission League championship."

Thurman watched the screen, gripping the pool stick by both hands as if he were strangling it, his face a mirror of burning hatred. He grabbed the pool stick by the end and smashed it against the pool table.

Chapter Twenty-Nine

Coach Ferrentini, smiling as the team celebrated its victory, waded through the locker room with his coaches, and made his way to his office. He stopped in the doorway when he saw Joe Meyers, a large cigar in his mouth, sitting with his feet propped up on his desk.

Red Meyers, still in uniform, nervously sat in a chair next to the desk.

Ferrentini turned to his coaches. "You guys leave. I'll handle this." He turned toward Joe Meyers.

"We gotta talk, Nick," Meyers said. "Shut the door!"

Ferrentini didn't say anything, first looking at Red whose face showed a wishful hopefulness, then at Joe, and then at Joe's feet on his desk.

"I was under the impression this was my office," Ferrentini said.

"Don't be such a wise-ass, Nick! I'm not one of your damn players!"

"Get your damn feet off my desk and put out that cigar!"

Red got up from his chair, but his dad didn't move.

"Listen, coach," Red said, "what you did out there was unfair."

"Shut up," Joe Meyers yelled at his son.

It was silent in the room for a moment as Joe Meyers took a draw on his cigar and looked at Ferrentini through a veil of smoke.

"You probably cost Red his record, Nick. Now, he's going to play next week, isn't he?"

Ferrentini pointed to a wall where a picture of a championship-winning team from two years ago was displayed.

"Do you see that picture, Joe? . . . Well, that is a football *team*! They won the championship because they played as a team. Your son forgot about that tonight, and our quarterback is being checked out in the hospital because your kid didn't do what was expected of him on the field. And I need to consider what the team expects of me when I decide whether or not he's going to play next week."

"When in hell did you become concerned about what the team thinks about you?"

Ferrentini pulled a set of keys from his pocket and threw them on the desk. They were the keys to the Jaguar he drove every day to school.

Meyers stared at them before looking back up at Ferrentini.

"Are you telling me that you're not going to start Red next week?"

"Good guess, Joe! You should've been a prophet. Now get your damn feet off my desk."

Joe Meyers got up and pointed his cigar at Ferrentini.

"You wanna know something, Ferrentini? Chances are real good you're not going to be here next year."

"And do you know what, Joe? If an arrogant son of a bitch like you can take my job away, it wasn't worth having in the first place. Now, get out of my office!"

Meyers stood up. "Come on boy. Let's get out of here!"

"Red's staying!" Ferrentini said. "I need to talk to him."

Meyers threw his lit cigar contemptuously in a wastebasket. "Come on boy! Let's go home!"

Before he got to the door, Joe Meyers turned to face Ferrentini. "I'm going to have your job for this! Do you hear me?"

"Joe, if Red walks out of here without talking to me, he's off the squad."

Red paused for a moment. He looked at the coach and then at his father. "Dad, I want to play football. I'll see you later."

Joe Meyers grabbed his son by the arm and led him out of the office.

Kai was the first to notice Tyler Jefferson when he walked into the locker room, a shirt draped over his shoulders and his bare chest bound up in tape. Kai nudged Angelo who turned and saw him.

Angelo's smile grew wider. "He's back."

"Not good for you."

Angelo's response didn't surprise Kai who by this time knew him well.

"He's our quarterback," Angelo continued. "I've learned a lot just by watching him play."

There was a loud cheer when the players saw Tyler come through the door into the locker room.

"Did I miss something?" Tyler said. "I heard we won the Mission League Championship. Break out the beer and dogs!"

The hills that gave Jefferson Heights its name curved in a half-circle that faced north. The ridge at the eastern end of the arc was higher than the others and had been flattened by excavators to create an acre of level ground that was now occupied by a palatial mansion owned by the parents of Tyler and Patty Jefferson.

At a quarter to eleven, three buses containing the Jefferson Heights football team and the cheerleaders pulled up in front of the two-story residence. When Kai got out of the bus, he looked around and could hardly believe what he saw. The mansion was larger than the one owned by the Meyers and the landscaping was Disneyland perfect. There was a large banner draped over the top floor of the structure that read, RED RAIDERS–TOMAHAWK THE WARRIORS.

"Impressive, isn't it?" Angelo said when he saw Kai staring at the mansion and its surroundings.

Kai nodded. "I didn't know that dentists could make that much money."

"Well, like I said, Mr. Jefferson owns a bunch of offices. Do you know who has the biggest house in the Heights?"

When Kai shook his head, Angelo said, "Roy Brice. Do you know how he started out?"

"I'm sure you'll tell me."

"He was a plumber."

Kai and Angelo followed the team along a landscaped path that led to a pool in the backyard that was sheltered from the winds by a six-foot glass wall. Off in the distance was the gleaming skyline of downtown Los Angeles.

For the first time that night, Kai thought of Thurman Adams. He was out there somewhere in the City. Kai wondered what he might be doing.

Tyler Jefferson's parents were cooking hotdogs and hamburgers by the pool with Patty acting as a server when Angelo and Kai got in line. Angelo's girlfriend, Marie, who was one of the cheerleaders, was hanging on his arm. Tyler Jefferson was in line in front of them.

Kai noticed a large container containing cans of Hires root beer on ice. He laughed. "Beer and dogs? This is beer and dogs? I thought we were having real beer."

"Root beer and hotdogs!" Angelo said. "It's their way of keeping us off the streets when we win a big one. What do you think they're doing tonight at Ignatius?"

"The team usually goes to Dinsie's," Kai replied.

Tyler Jefferson turned around to listen to the conversation.

"What's Dingy's?" Marie asked.

It was the first time that Kai had gotten this close to Marie. She was extraordinarily thin but managed to be well-proportioned. Her cheerleader's uniform showed off her shapely legs.

"It's Dinsie's, not Dingy's. That's where the grunts from Ignatius go to blow off steam after they win a game. They'd drink enough beer to spend the rest of the night with their head in a toilet if Coach Lindsey didn't put a stop to it."

"You're kidding, aren't you?" Tyler said.

"On no. It's for real," Kai said. "The grunts all know when the Coach and Father Mike are coming. They have lookouts and they try to find some way to slow 'em down."

The burger stand called Dinsie's had a huge butcher-paper banner flying on the roof scrawled with, GO WARRIORS–FLATTEN THE HEIGHTS. The lot behind the burger stand was crowded with cars and people.

A large crowd of students solemnly watched the football team as it circled in the throes of the tribal dance.

Five blocks away, Father Mike and Coach Lindsey were drinking a beer from cans inside Father Mike's sedan. Coach Lindsey looked at his watch.

"Time to break up the party?" Father Mike asked.

Lindsey nodded his head. "It's time."

Father Mike's car peeled out of the lot and raced down Maple Avenue, passing two parked police cars. The police cars turned on their emergency lights and took off in pursuit, sirens screaming,

Father Mike's car was parked at the curb with two police cars angled behind it. He and Coach Lindsey were on the sidewalk. Coach Lindsey was leaning against the car, smoking a cigar. Father McKay stared at the two police officers who were near the open door of one of the police cars. The officers were desperately trying to keep from laughing.

"What are they doing?" Father Mike asked, a perturbed look on his face. "They're laughing at us, aren't they?"

"They're running warrant checks on us," Lindsey replied. "I hope you don't have any unpaid tickets."

"Warrant checks! Why warrant checks? They must know who we are."

"Of course, they do. They played football for me not more than ten years ago."

"What?"

"You heard what I said."

"I'll have a talk with them."

Coach Lindsey stopped him with a wave of the hand.

"Be careful, Mike. Those police cars have video cameras, so don't say anything you wouldn't want to see on television next week. The Bishop won't be happy, and you'll lose any chance of ever becoming pope."

Patty Jefferson, wearing a miniskirt that showed she was wearing a zebra-striped bikini when she bent over, dropped a hotdog onto Tyler's plate. When she looked up and saw Tyler in front of her, she took the hotdog back. She broke a large piece off and dropped the smaller piece onto Tyler's plate.

"I forgot you take a small one."

The players in line broke up laughing.

Angered, Tyler grabbed three hotdogs from the tray and slapped them onto his plate. "Patty, I've just about had it with you!"

"You never had it with me, and lucky for me you never will!"

More laughing, this time louder. Tyler's face looked like he fell into a patch of poison ivy. He sputtered for a moment and then hurled an insult at her.

"Zipperfish!"

"Oh, look at mister teenie-weenie talking."

When Angelo and Kai stepped in front of Patty, her face broke into a mischievous smile.

"Well, if it isn't the bruise brothers." She nodded at Tyler who was moving down the line. "Old numbnuts here can't take a little hit on the football field without having his little firecracker checked out by a doctor."

Doctor and Mrs. Jefferson joined Patty in the serving line, both wearing oversized chefs' hats. If Patty's brain was one click off-center, Mrs. Jefferson's brain was two clicks off. She wore a battered sweatshirt with a cartoon of a smiling, maroon-faced Indian plunging a hatchet into the head of a goofy-looking Indian wearing a halo. The smile on her face was slightly less goofy than the Indian's on her sweatshirt.

"Hi-ho, Angelo," Doctor Jefferson said. "Great game!"

"You did a great job filling in for Tyler tonight," Mrs. Jefferson said, the sound of her voice sounding like a mouse's squeak.

Kai cast a sideways glance at Angelo.

Angelo's smile grew wider. "Well, I tried my best. Thank you for having us over."

"And halloooo, Kai. You had a fantastic game. We're glad you could join us."

"Thank you, Mr. Jefferson."

"I bet they don't have anything like this at Saint Ignatius," Mrs. Jefferson said.

"You're right, ma'am. They have nothing like this at Saint Ignatius!"

Chapter Thirty

Frank Johnson, the night security guard at Saint Ignatius, was conscientious. He walked the ground and checked each of the buildings on the campus eight times a night. It was on his second walk-through the dimly lit gymnasium that he heard a crashing sound coming from the football team's locker room. He stopped and listened. Hearing nothing further, he loosened the pistol in its holster and cautiously approached the locker room door.

The only light in the locker room came through the windows that were high up on the north wall. Johnson pulled a flashlight out of his jacket pocket and stepped inside. When he tried to turn it on, it wouldn't work.

Another loud crash came from the far side of the locker room. Johnson shook his flashlight and it unexpectedly came on. He pointed it in the direction of the sound and saw that the door to the football equipment room was partially open.

Approaching the door, he removed his semi-automatic pistol from the holster.

He called out, "Who's there?"

His flashlight went out. He muttered a curse.

There was another crash, this one louder, this one closer.

Johnson moved cautiously through the door into the equipment room. His eyes were drawn to the left. Pale light streamed through a barred window. He looked to the right. The last thing he saw in his life was a blast of gunfire into his face.

Early Saturday morning, Coach Lindsey watched his team taking laps around the athletic field next to the gymnasium where several police cars were parked.

Sergeant Sid Conners came out of the gym and approached Lindsey.

"Okay, Sherlock," Lindsey said, "have you solved this case yet?"

Before Conners could answer, a player stopped in front of them and vomited. It set off a chain reaction among the players and Lindsey and Conners stepped back to keep their shoes from being splattered.

"Damn, Eddie! What are you trying to do?" Conners said. "They look like hell." He scowled when he saw another player throwing up.

"It's called God's justice, Sid. They're repenting for the sins of last night."

Conners gave Lindsey a strange look before speaking again.

What in the hell did he mean by God's justice?

"Eddie, I need some help here."

"What kind of help?"

"Are you sure it wasn't one of your players that did this killing? I mean, not all of them are altar boys, are they?"

"Sid, you played ball here, didn't you? Ever hear of Dinsie's?"

"Who hasn't? Back in my time, no one had a burning desire to do a godforsaken war dance in the middle of the night."

"All of those boys out there were at Dinsie's last night, Sid," he said, pointing to the players running around the field. "Your buddies in uniform were running interference for them last night while my boys were drinking enough beer to float a battleship." Lindsey paused for a moment, looking thoughtful. "And tell me this, Sid. Why would they want to break into the locker room when they have access to it all day long?"

"I'm not getting any cooperation from your equipment manager. He claims he doesn't know if anything was taken."

"I already told you that. The only thing we have in there is athletic equipment. A lot of it gets thrown away when it gets damaged. So, we don't know what we have in there until everyone checks in their gear at the end of the season."

Conners frowned. "Okay, coach. I'm going to ask you a favor. I want you to survey your players and see what equipment they have in their possession, and then compare it with the record in the equipment room, and then with the inventory you had at the start of the year."

"Aren't you a little over-reacting, Sid? That's a tall order."

"I'm investigating a murder, coach."

"Look, it doesn't make any sense that anyone would steal football equipment. There's no logic to it."

"Since when is there a logic to murder, coach?"

Another player broke out of the line and vomited too close to Conners. He backed away, shaking muck from his shoes.

On Monday afternoon, the Jefferson Heights football team was sitting on the ground at the practice field stretching their muscles before scrimmaging. Tyler Jefferson's face winced in pain every time he tried to touch his toes.

Kai noticed Angelo was watching him with interest.

"There goes your chance to play in the big one on Friday night, Angelo," Kai said. "I think he's going to be ready to play."

"We need him to win, Kai. I haven't had a chance to practice all of our plays, and we'll need every one of them against Saint Ignatius."

A loud bang echoed across the field. Kai whipped his head around in alarm. It sounded like a gunshot. His sudden concern dissolved into a smile when he saw a battered pickup, emitting black smoke and crawling on its last legs into a parking space reserved for the coaches.

He watched as Ferrentini got out of the truck with an unpleasant look on his face.

"Big Red took the Jag away from him," Angelo said to Kai.

As Ferrentini walked toward the practice field, the pickup truck started dieseling, its motor rumbling in protest on superheated fumes. He stared at it with a lethal gaze until it stopped.

Ferrentini walked up to Coach Casey who had trouble suppressing a smile.

"Damn thing needs a tune-up," Ferrentini said casually. "It's been sitting in the garage for three years." He looked at Casey uneasily. "Did he show up?"

"Who? . . . Red? Hell no."

Ferrentini appeared distracted.

Casey watched him curiously. "You don't really plan on playing him after what he did to Tyler, do you?"

"Let's break out into practice groups and run our drills."

The coaches issued their orders and the players got up and began to disperse. Kai and Angelo followed the scout team.

Ferrentini squinted into the late afternoon sun. "Hey Moore, where in the hell do you think you're going?"

Kai and Angelo stopped and looked back.

"Over with Coach Prince, sir," Kai responded.

"Get your butt over with first string offense."

Kai smiled. "Yes, sir."

Later, Kai was with the offensive unit in a huddle waiting for the coaches to decide what play to run when Oliver Brown called their attention to a player coming onto the field.

"Omigod! Lookey, lookey who's here!" Brown said.

The team turned and saw Red Meyers jogging up to the huddle.

"Hi guys. Ol' Red is back." Red said with a smile on his face.

Not one of the players returned his smile.

Moose Basich, the left guard, stepped forward and grabbed Red by the front of his jersey. "Listen here, shithead, you miss one more block, and I will pound your ass so far into the ground they're gonna need an escalator to dig you out."

Moose flung Red to the ground like a rag doll.

Ferrentini saw Red lying sprawled on the ground and quickly intervened. "What are you doin' down there?"

"Moose hit me!"

Moose was quick to reply. "Bullshit!"

Ferrentini looked at Moose and then back at Red Meyers. "Get in the huddle!"

Red got up, went back to the huddle, and took a position next to Kai.

"Not that huddle Meyers," Ferrentini said. "You're working out with the scout team today."

Red stared at Ferrentini for a moment and then turned to go downfield.

After Red had left, Tyler Jefferson tapped Kai on the shoulder. "Looks like you'll be starting Friday night, Moore. Congratulations."

"Did you hear what Moose said about an escalator?" Kai asked. "How do you dig someone out of the ground with an escalator?"

Tyler smiled. "Beats me. You have to remember he's a lineman. They use comic books to show linemen how to run plays."

On the day before the game with Saint Ignatius, Edna McKay knocked softly on Kai's bedroom door.

"Kai, are you still in bed. There's a phone call for you."

Kai sat up in bed. "What?"

"The phone . . . it's for you."

Kai, sleepy-eyed, quickly dressed and headed for the kitchen. He picked up the phone. "Hello?"

A familiar voice came on the line, a voice Kai recognized.

"Did I wake you?"

It was Denise, his girlfriend . . . or maybe his girlfriend . . . he hadn't seen her for almost nine months. He sat down at the kitchen table.

"Denise?"

"Yes, it's Denise. How many Denise's do you know?"

"What's wrong?"

"Nothing's wrong. I just wanted to talk to you. Okay?"

Kai thought she sounded exasperated. He scratched his head.

"Will you be at the game tomorrow night?" he asked.

"Yes. Will you?"

Kai nodded his head vigorously. "Yes. It looks like I'll be starting at tailback."

There was a long pause on the line before Denise responded.

"That's real good, Ryan . . . or is it Kai now? Anyway, I'm glad for you."

"I'm almost afraid to ask," Kai said hesitantly. "Are you going out with anyone?"

"Yes, I am . . . some football player by the name of Ryan Moore, but he hasn't been around lately. Do you know him?"

"I think I've heard of him before."

"I have a car now. Maybe we can meet after the game."

"What about your parents? Will they let you?"

"Of course."

"What changed their mind?"

"I think Sergeant Conners talked to them. Dad told me he felt sorry for you, and it was Mom who suggested I call you."

It was now Denise's turn to hesitate. "Are *you* going out with anyone?"

"Yes. I mean no. Yes, I'm not going out with anyone. The only girls I know here are a little strange."

"Do you know Patty Jefferson?"

"She sits right next to me in Journalism. How do you know her?"

"Patty's a legend. Did you hear how she got kicked off the cheerleader squad?"

"I heard, but I'm not sure I believe it."

"Well, it did happen. She flashed the other team with her . . . well, you know what I'm talking about."

Kai thought he could actually hear her blush.

"She already told me what she did."

"How do you feel about playing against your buddies tomorrow?"

"I think about them a lot."

"I know they're thinking about you too. But not in their prayers!"

Kai smiled.

"Ryan, I have to run. I'm looking forward to seeing you tomorrow night."

"I'm looking forward to seeing you, too." He was thinking how strange it was for someone to be using his given name. He sort of liked the name Kai better.

"Everyone at school is saying that Thurman Adams is looking for you. You need to be real careful."

There was a long silence on the phone.

"Ryan? Are you there?"

"Yes?"

"Just because I like you a lot, don't get the wrong idea. I hope Saint Ignatius kicks the butt off Jefferson Heights tomorrow night."

There was a soft click on the phone as Denise hung up.

The Final Chapter

Kai walked into the locker room wearing black dress slacks, and a white long-sleeved shirt with a scarlet tie. A few players in identical dress were already in the locker room. Kai went to the bulletin board next to Ferrentini's office and saw the lineup for the game, STARTING SQUADS FOR SAINT IGNATIUS. Kai's name was listed on the kick-off and punt return teams and at running back. He whistled softly.

Jefferson Heights versus Saint Ignatius at City Stadium.

Six school buses containing the football team, the band, and cheerleaders pulled out of the lot at Jefferson Heights High School. A large group of parents and students who were on the sidewalk cheered as the buses headed down the street. The caravan was led and followed by a large police and security guard escort.

As the caravan passed through Jefferson Heights, Kai looked pensively up at the hill where Thurman took a shot at him. He turned in his seat when he felt something imaginary crawling on his neck and saw Red Meyers, a few seats back, glaring at him.

Red looked away.

Just outside of downtown Los Angeles, Thurman Adams, a rattlesnake in search of a victim, emerged from the warehouse carrying a large duffle bag. He tossed the bag in the rear of a broken-down pick-up truck he had stolen from the City Produce Market and got into the cab. He started the truck and drove slowly down the alley.

Sid Conners along with two uniformed officers watched as the ticket takers opened the gate to City Stadium and let the anxious crowd in. Several dozen kids scrambled into the stadium. One of them, a tall Black kid with a semi-Afro, caused a police officer to look at a photo of Thurman Adams concealed in the palm of his hand.

Conners caught his eye and shook his head, 'no.'

Two bus convoys containing the opposing teams simultaneously entered the stadium parking lot from two different entrances and proceeded to the locker room area. Security personnel and police officers jumped out of their vehicles and formed a cordon around the buses as the teams begin unloading. The Saint Ignatius team, led by Coach Lindsey and Father Mike McKay, were wearing blue slacks, white shirts, and ties.

The players from both teams glared at each other from across the lot as they headed to their respective locker rooms. Several Saint Ignatius players gave Kai the gangster stare when they saw him.

Kai ignored them, his face expressionless.

One hour later, the Jefferson Heights band, accompanied by cheerleaders and flag girls, were on the field playing a furious marching tune. The Jefferson Heights fans waved a V-sign in rhythm with the beat, while the Jefferson Heights Red Raiders and the Saint Ignatius Warriors formed up on either side of the end zones.

The crowd began to roar when they saw the teams. The sound was so loud that Kai, standing alongside Angelo, had to yell to make himself heard.

"Awesome isn't it?"

"Awesome!" Angelo agreed. He noticed Kai looking in the direction of the Saint Ignatius cheerleaders. "Which one is she?"

"The prettiest one."

Angelo started to say something, but his voice was drowned out by the stadium announcer.

"Ladies and gentlemen, welcome to the championship game of the Mission League. Entering the field at the west end are the Red Raiders of Jefferson Heights."

The Jefferson Heights team swarmed onto the field accompanied by the roar of their fans and the boos of Saint Ignatius.

In the bleachers, Edna McKay stood quietly, a proud look on her face.

Joe Meyers, an obscene cigar in his mouth, looked on sourly.

Patty Jefferson, wearing a flimsy blouse and a mini skirt with tan knee-length boots, bounced up and down so much that her boobs came within inches of her chin.

Sid Conners in the broadcast booth began scanning the crowd with binoculars.

After the coin toss, the referee signaled that Jefferson Heights would receive the ball. A cheer erupted from the fans of both teams.

A minute later, Coach Lindsey entered the huddle on the sideline with his highly charged kick-off team and put one hand on the shoulder of his kicker.

"Massey, tell me again. What are you going to do out there?"

"In field kick, away from Moore."

"That's right, that's right." Lindsey looked at each player in turn and then said, "When you go out there, make a statement and make it huge! Get downfield fast! Stick it to the runner as hard as you can. Give that team a serious impression of what it's like to play football with the Warriors. Do you understand me?"

The kick-off squad responded with a loud, "Yes, sir!"

Kai Moore and Paul Bishop took up positions at the twenty-yard line. The referee blew the whistle and Saint Ignatius kicked off.

The ball was kicked deep to Bishop's side of the field, and he circled back to catch it. Kai rushed over to cover his back in case he dropped it.

There was no need.

Bishop caught the ball and ran up the field behind a blocking wedge that formed up in front of him.

Mere seconds later, Saint Ignatius crashed into the wedge with the intensity of a herd of mad bulls. Bishop slowed for a moment, looking for a way around the players, and the hesitation cost him. One player, who had been knocked to the ground, reached out and grabbed him by the legs. Bishop turned away, trying to break free, and saw Kai coming up behind him. He tossed the ball to Kai who caught the ball in full stride.

Kai broke sharply to the left toward the Saint Ignatius sideline and eluded the entire defensive team. He skimmed the sideline with the kick-off team in pursuit.

The Saint Ignatius players on the sideline were hysterically yelling, "Get him, get him!"

Kai sprinted into the end zone a few seconds later.

Up in the broadcast booth. the announcer was ecstatic. "And just like that, with only twelve seconds into the game, Jefferson Heights 6, Saint Ignatius nothing! Moore scores on a lateral from Bishop."

The Jefferson Heights crowd went wild, but on the Saint Ignatius sideline, Kai's girlfriend, Denise, bit her lower lip.

A fellow cheerleader walked up to her and stared at her, face-to-face. "Denise, don't you even dare smile!"

Despite Denise's best effort, a glimmer of a smile broke through. The other cheerleader walked away in disgust.

Outside the stadium, a dingy pickup truck wound its way through the semi-darkness of the parking lot and pulled into an open space. The driver, Thurman Adams, had the radio on and had just heard the announcer in a high-pitched voice report that Kai Moore had scored a touchdown for Jefferson Heights. For one brief moment, Thurman felt as if he was going to be sick.

He lowered his head for a moment, his mind temporarily occupied with the thought that he might be catching a cold, not realizing that the cause of his sudden nausea might be his burning desire to kill Kai Moore.

After a moment, Thurman settled down. He got out of the truck. The cool air refreshed his mind and he felt better. He looked toward the brightly lit stadium when he heard a cheer rise up from one side of the field.

Cheer all you want, assholes, Thurman thought. *Wait until you see what I've got for you.*

Thurman dragged the duffle bag out of the bed of the truck and opened it. The first thing he pulled out of the bag was Terry Lewis' semi-automatic pistol.

Things weren't going well for Saint Ignatius. They received the ball on the kick-off in decent field position but were unable to move the ball and had to kick on fourth down.

The Saint Ignatius punter booted a high one, and Kai came under it, signaling for a fair catch. Three Ignatius players put on the brakes and stopped less than two yards away from Kai as he caught the ball.

The players walked past Kai, glaring at him. One of them brushed his elbow against his left arm provocatively. Kai let it go but stopped when he heard his birth name being called by one of the Saint Ignatius players.

"Hey, Ryan!"

Kai turned to look. A Saint Ignatius linebacker named Charlie Nichols was coming onto the field. His greeting seemed friendly enough. Kai returned it.

"Hey, Charlie!"

Nichols had a big grin on his meaty face. "I like your colors, Ryan, red . . . blood red . . . the color of what's going to be running all over this here field tonight."

Kai started to say something, but he saw an official watching. He jogged over to the offensive huddle where an angry Moose Basich tapped him on the shoulder.

"Did that punk threaten you?"

"I don't know, Moose. He's a linebacker. I don't speak primitive languages."

Jefferson Heights broke out of the huddle. The Saint Ignatius defensive unit glared at Kai as he calmly took his position in the backfield.

Tyler Jefferson stooped down under center to take the ball.

Charlie Nichols began yelling, "Trips left, trips left!"

The Ignatius defensive unit took up the cry, and Tyler Jefferson realizing the defense was momentarily distracted rushed through the cadence.

"Ready! Set! Set!"

The rushed cadence didn't faze Kai. He took the ball on a hand-off from Tyler and ran into heavy traffic over the right side. He reversed direction, dodged a tackler, and ran right over another.

Rounding the tight end, Kai turned upfield.

Nichols, the middle linebacker, slipped through the blocking and rushed in for the tackle.

Moose Basich raced toward Nichols like a heat-seeking missile and blindsided him so hard that his helmet flew off.

Kai vaulted over the stunned Nichols and raced downfield for his second touchdown.

The scoreboard immediately changed. Jefferson Heights 13, Saint Ignatius 0. There were nine minutes left on the clock in the first quarter.

In the end zone, Kai gave Moose Basich a high five. Moose had other ideas. He gave Kai a rib-crushing hug.

On his way to the bench, Kai passed Charlie Nichols as he was slowly getting up from the ground. Nichols snatched his helmet off the ground and angrily wiped away a rivulet of blood streaming from his elbow.

Kai paused to look at him.

"Charlie, you were right about blood running on the field. Only it ain't mine."

"That run ain't for shit, Moore!" Nichols said as he put his helmet back on. "Wait until you see what we got for you."

Kai smiled and pretended as if he was wiping blood off his elbow.

Saint Ignatius finally caught on fire. Two minutes later, their fullback ran off center, broke a tackle by Buster Hollister, and scored on a thirty-five-yard run.

The Saint Ignatius crowd came to life as the scoreboard changed: Jefferson Heights 14, Saint Ignatius 6.

On the kick-off, Paul Bishop caught the ball and ran eighteen yards before being brought down. Jefferson Heights now had the ball on their twenty-nine-yard line.

And nobody, except for two alert security guards on the sideline, noticed a tall Saint Ignatius player, wearing number 89 on a loose-fitting jersey, enter the stadium from the Warrior locker room and jog toward the team bench. As he jogged past the two security guards, they stared at his spidery legs.

The security guards were Black, both retired from the U.S. Air Force. They looked at each other.

One of them said, "Do you know that boy?"

"I know he's got a problem."

"Oh?"

"He's got the skinniest legs I've ever seen. If he had an Afro under that helmet, he'd look like a Q-tip."

They watched as number 89 entered the Saint Ignatius team area and inched his way through the players to the sideline.

"I think," the other guard replied, "we better find that Conners guy. I don't like the way that boy is sneaking about."

On the sideline, Thurman Adams hauled up his jersey and adjusted the semi-automatic pistol tucked in his pants. He nudged a Saint Ignatius player standing in front of him.

"Which one of them dawgs is Moore?"

"Number 27."

The player turned around to look at Adams. "Who duh hell are you?"

Before he could answer, Thurman caught a glimpse of a running play coming directly toward the sideline. He stood on his toes, trying to get a better look at the runner.

He spotted him. It was number 27. He was being pursued by three players, and they were heading in his direction.

Thurman reached for his gun.

An assistant coach yelled, "Get back! Get back!"

The players on the sidelines were unable to get away in time and the runners crashed into them.

Thurman was knocked back by the collision and lost his balance. He recovered in time to see number 27 returning to the huddle on the field. Now was his big chance to get the little bastard. A chance to get revenge for Calvin and Billy.

He stepped onto the field, fingering the semi-automatic pistol in his waistband. He didn't see the chain crew running along the sideline to mark the first down. The lead man collided into Thurman, nearly knocking him down. When Thurman recovered his balance, a member of the chain crew thrust the down marker forcefully into the ground in front of Thurman's face.

An official on the field yelled at Thurman. "Get back behind the lines number 89 and let these men set the chains."

Thurman grunted but did as he was told. He didn't like the way things were going. This was nothing like he had planned. He stepped back and continued to look on the field for number 27, not noticing that a trainer was staring at him.

The trainer approached Coach Lindsey and Father McKay. "Coach, who's number 89?" He pointed towards Thurman.

Coach Lindsey's face took on an expression of horror. "My God! How did he get in here?" He turned to one of his assistant coaches. "Find Sergeant Conners and tell him Thurman Adams is here."

Lindsey turned to look at Thurman. The thug was watching the game. He was also wearing a team uniform, which he must have stolen from the team equipment room last weekend.

He began wondering if he shouldn't organize the coaches to take him down, but he also remembered that a security guard had been murdered last weekend, and it was likely that Thurman Adams was the one who killed him. And that also meant that Thurman Adams was carrying a gun under his uniform jersey.

Lindsey turned his attention back to the field where Kai blocked for Tyler Jefferson as he dropped back and threw an incomplete pass.

The Saint Ignatius' security supervisor approached Coach Lindsey.

"I think you should know. My men saw a funny-looking player entering the team area."

"Where's Conners?" Lindsey asked.

"I think he's in the stands."

"Get him. Tell him that our player number 89 is Thurman Adams."

"What? Where?"

"Do what I said — *now!*"

"Coach, I can handle him. Where is he?"

"Do what I said and do it now! And get someone over to Ferrentini and tell him to pull Kai Moore from the game!"

On the field, Tyler pitched the ball to Kai who swept left. As Kai rounded the corner, he got a brief glimpse of a tall skinny Black player on the sideline as he turned up field.

Kai picked up fifteen yards before he was tackled near the sideline.

Thurman plunged his way through the players on the sideline to the thirty-three-yard-line, where Kai was knocked down, but found he was no longer there.

In the broadcast booth, a security officer grabbed Conners by the arm and whispered in his ear. Conners grabbed his binoculars and scanned the Saint Ignatius bench.

On the field, Kai looked over the top of the Jefferson Heights huddle toward the Saint Ignatius bench. The tall Back player that he saw when he swept by the Saint Ignatius bench looked awfully familiar.

"Moore!"

Tyler was speaking to him.

"Listen up! I'm calling a play and you're not paying attention."

Kai brought his attention back to the huddle to find his team staring at him.

"I'm sorry Tyler. I thought I saw Thurman Adams on the Ignatius bench."

"Who in the hell is Thurman Adams?" Oliver Brown asked.

"That's the dude that killed his mother," another player said.

There was an embarrassed silence in the huddle.

"Do you need to take a breather?" Tyler asked Kai.

"No!" He almost shouted out the response, and then said quietly, "Call your play."

On the Jefferson Heights sideline, a security officer approached Ferrentini.

"Coach!"

"What? Who're you? What the hell are you doin' in my team box?"

"I have a message from Coach Lindsey," the security officer said. "He wants you to pull Moore from the game."

Ferrentini exploded. "Yeah, I'll bet he does. Get your sorry ass out of here!"

Using two players as cover, Thurman Adams removed the semi-automatic pistol from under his jersey. He pulled open the slide to make sure a round was chambered. Two players saw what he was doing and backed away.

Sergeant Sid Conners clumsily vaulted over the fence onto the track behind the Saint Ignatius bench. He tapped Coach Lindsey on the shoulder.

"Where is he?" Conners asked.

Lindsey pointed down the sideline.

Thurman was no longer there.

"He was standing there just a few seconds ago," Lindsey said. "He was wearing a uniform."

"What number?"

"It was 89."

Without saying another word, Conners began a frantic search through the crowd of players on the sideline.

On the field, the Jefferson Heights broke out of the huddle. Tyler Jefferson had called a passing play that called for two wide receivers.

Kai took a semi-standing position with his body bent slightly forward behind the fullback.

In the Saint Ignatius secondary, player number 89 lined up halfway between Charlie Nichols and the defensive end. Nichols angrily stepped forward and grabbed him by the shoulder.

"Hey man, you're outta position!"

Thurman turned and stared at Nichols with a maniacal look on his face.

Nichols didn't like what he saw in those hate-filled eyes.

He quickly backed away.

From his position in the backfield, Kai saw Nichols warily backing away from a player with the number 89 on his jersey. When the player turned to face the line, Kai found himself staring into the face of Thurman Adams.

Thurman glared at him, his eyes on fire with hatred.

Kai hesitated for just a second. He straightened up and called out to Tyler. "Check! Check!"

Tyler turned from his position behind the center.

"Thirty-four blast, thirty-four blast!" Kai continued.

Tyler nodded. He turned to the left and then right, calling out the play. "Check! Check! Thirty-four blast, thirty-four blast! Quick, quick!"

The offensive line shifted tight and the two wide receivers moved closer.

In the Saint Ignatius backfield, Thurman pulled the gun out from under his jersey.

Nichols frantically looked at the bench and pointed his finger in a jabbing motion at Thurman.

On the sideline, Coach Lindsey grabbed his defensive coordinator by the shoulder.

"We've got twelve men on the field! Who snuck out there on us?"

Conners, a few feet away, whipped his head towards the field.

Lindsey yelled out to Nichols. "For God's sake, call a timeout, call a timeout!"

Nichols didn't hear him. His eyes were frozen on the player wearing number 89.

On the field, Kai took a half-crouched stance and locked eyes with Thurman's. He watched as Thurman pulled a gun out from underneath his jersey.

Tyler yelled out, "Set!"

The ball was snapped.

Kai rocketed out of his position and took the hand-off from Tyler. He followed the fullback Morris to the line of scrimmage, aiming for a gap between the left tackle and left guard. The outside linebacker rushed in to close the gap and was promptly flattened by Morris.

Thurman's eyes were terror-stricken at the unexpected violence. He froze as he saw the offensive line crash forcefully into the defense, splitting a hole between the tackle and the guard. An outside linebacker rushed in to close the gap but was knocked down by the fullback who went down with him.

Kai leaped over the linebacker and the fullback. He lowered his head and drove his helmet into Thurman's solar plexus, knocking him off his feet.

Thurman dropped the gun as he fell backward, his arms flailing helplessly. Kai drove him into the ground as hard as he could.

Several Saint Ignatius players piled on top of Kai to make sure he was down.

At the bottom of the pile, Kai was face-to-face with Thurman Adams whose eyes were glazed over with pain.

"Welcome to Red Raiders football . . . you damn fool!"

As Kai got up, he deliberately slipped and dropped a knee into Thurman's stomach.

The impact caused Thurman's lungs to deflate with a sudden whoosh, and he began to groan.

The umpire rushed up and looked down at Thurman. He signaled a timeout.

Kai walked away, a grim smile on his face.

Conners and Lindsey rushed out onto the field. Conners knelt and patted down Thurman's waist for the gun.

None was there.

Frantically, Conners looked around and spotted the semi-automatic on the ground. He grabbed it and put it in his pocket.

The umpire looked in. "What was that?"

"Get a stretcher out here," Conners said. "This boy is hurt!"

The umpire spotted a pair of handcuffs tucked in Conners' belt.

"Who are you?"

Coach Lindsey spoke up. "Listen, buddy, this is our doctor. Let him do his job!"

The umpire shrugged and walked away.

Conners rolled Thurman over and handcuffed him. He quickly turned Thurman on his back to conceal the cuffs.

Kai entered the Jefferson Heights team huddle.

"Okay, what was that all about?" Tyler asked Kai. "Why did you bust that dude's grill?"

"That was the guy that killed my mother."

It was quiet for a moment as the players looked at Kai. Then Moose Basich spoke up, winning the prize for the dumbest comment ever made on a football field.

"Damn, they let anybody play on these teams from the ghetto, don't they!"

There was a scattering of light applause as Thurman was carried off the field accompanied by Conners.

On the stretcher, Thurman looked around quizzically.

"That's for you Adams," Conners said. "That's about the only time in your godforsaken life you're gonna get applause from anybody."

Thurman tried to get up but then realized he was handcuffed.

"I should put your ass back into that football game," Conners continued, "and let you bang around with those boys some more."

Father Mike joined Conners as two paramedics were placing Thurman into an ambulance.

"Is he seriously hurt?" Father Mike asked.

"He may have a few broken ribs," Conners said. "Too bad we don't have the death penalty anymore. It had a way of curing pain real quick."

"But he's a juvenile. They never gave the death penalty to a juvenile."

"He's no longer a juvenile. He turned eighteen last month." Conners showed Father Mike the semi-automatic he picked up from the ground. "A gun like this was used to kill your security guard last weekend. I'm pretty sure this belongs to one of our detectives who turned up missing. By the time I get this asshole to the hospital, I'll know what he did to him."

Conners climbed into the ambulance.

Father Mike, a grim look on his face, watched the ambulance drive off.

The public address announcer brought his attention back to the game.

"The referee has blown the ball ready for play and here come the Red Raiders."

A few minutes later, Kai swept around the end for a gain of twelve yards. He made it to the two-yard line before he was knocked out of bounds by a safety.

On the sideline, Coach Lindsey turned away from the field with a sour look on his face. He was not wearing his fedora.

On the Jefferson Heights sideline, Coach Ferrentini yelled out to his team. "Dive, dive."

On the next play, Kai blasted through the defensive line for a touchdown.

The scoreboard showed Jefferson Heights was up 20 to 7.

With four minutes left in the second quarter, the Red Raiders blitzed the Saint Ignatius' quarterback. He got off a pass under pressure, but the ball got tipped high into the air.

Buster Hollister caught the ball and ran thirty yards for a touchdown. Holding the ball high in the air, Buster pranced around in the end zone like a buffalo doing a war dance.

The public address announcer reported what everybody had already seen but added something that most people didn't know.

"Touchdown, Red Raiders. Lucius Hollister with the interception and the touchdown."

On the sideline, Kai and Angelo looked at each other in disbelief.

"Did you know his first name was Lucius?" Kai asked.

"Naw! That has to be a mistake." Angelo paused for a moment. "Do you think?"

In the third quarter, Kai, breaking tackles, plunged up the middle, made a fool of Charlie Nichols by making a sharp cut, and then ran forty-four yards for a touchdown.

Denise, a smile on her face, began to politely applaud but froze when she realized what she was doing. She laughed at herself to the consternation of her fellow cheerleaders.

At the start of the fourth quarter, Jefferson Heights wide receiver Paul Bishop caught a pass on the fly and scored a touchdown.

On the Saint Ignatius sideline, Coach Lindsey studied the heavens for a sign of relief. Father Mike looked like he was interested in something on the ground.

Saint Ignatius bobbled the ball on the following kick-off, and it was recovered by Jefferson Heights. On the next play, Kai faked blocking for Tyler for a beat and then dashed into the secondary. He turned to face Tyler and caught a short pass. Kai spun around as Charlie Nichols leaped through the air in the spot Kai had just vacated. Kai put on the afterburners and scored another touchdown.

In the Jefferson Heights stands, Edna McKay had lost all of her composure as she happily hugged a complete stranger.

Near the end of the game, the scoreboard showed Jefferson Heights 56, Saint Ignatius 24. There was 3:48 left to play in the game and a timeout had just been called.

From the huddle, Kai caught a glimpse of Red Meyers on the sideline. Red stood alone, disconsolate, staring at the scoreboard. A look of pity crossed Kai's face.

He turned his attention to Coach Ferrentini who had just entered the huddle.

"Okay, boys, let's head for home. Tyler, you call the rest of the game. Keep the ball on the ground." Ferrentini looked at Kai. "Moore, keep the ball in play and hold on to it. We don't need but four or five yards per carry to run the clock out."

Kai nodded and then asked, "Coach, what about Meyers?"

A look of astonishment crossed Ferrentini's face. "What about Meyers?"

"If he finishes the game, he still might have a chance to break the rushing record before the season is over."

Oliver Brown stepped forward and said to Ferrentini, "Sir, Meyers can shove that record up his ass!"

Ferrentini paused for a moment and then turned to Tyler. "Tyler, what do you think?"

Tyler glanced at Kai to see if he was serious.

Kai mouthed the word, "Angelo."

"Let him play, coach," Tyler said. "But Angelo deserves a shot. Let him finish the game."

Ferrentini paused for a beat. He turned and called across the field to Coach Prince. "Wally, get Meyers and Rodriguez in here on the double."

Kai and Tyler started to leave the huddle, but Ferrentini held up a hand and said, "Not yet."

They waited until Meyers and Rodriguez approached the huddle.

"Okay, now you two can leave," Ferrentini said.

As Tyler and Kai left the huddle for the sideline, the public address announcer came on the line.

"In for Jefferson at quarterback is Rodriguez. In for Moore at halfback is Meyers."

The Jefferson Heights fans rose to their feet and began an electrifying cheer as Kai and Tyler were greeted by their enthusiastic teammates.

When they were on the sideline, Tyler turned to Kai.

"Do you think that cheer was for us or Meyers?"

Kai laughed, but there were tears in his eyes.

On the field, the Jefferson Heights offense broke out of the huddle. At the snap, Angelo pitched out to Meyers who swept the end for a ten-yard gain before being hit hard.

On the sideline, Kai looked across the field to Denise, but she was busy with her fellow cheerleaders. He turned and looked up into the bleachers. A trace of sadness crossed his face, knowing that his mother was not there to see what he had accomplished.

A sudden movement caught his attention behind the players. He saw Patty Jefferson on the track behind the bench.

She smiled at him and pantomimed pulling up her blouse.

Kai vigorously shook his head, "No."

She pulled up her blouse, and a roar went up from the stands.

Two security officers rushed up and dragged Patty off by the arms. She protested but she let them lead her back into the spectator area.

Kai shook his head in amazement. He looked up into the bleachers and saw Edna McKay waving at him. He waved back.

Minutes later, the enthusiastic Jefferson Heights fans began loudly counting down.

"Ten, nine, eight . . ."

Kai looked out onto the field. The Jefferson Heights offense was at the four-yard line in a standing position waiting for the clock to run down. Angelo, standing proudly behind the center, had a broader smile on his face than Kai had ever seen. Red Meyers, standing at the running back position, looked as unhappy as the Saint Ignatius defense.

The public address announcer joined in the countdown. "Four, three, two, one! Jefferson Heights will be representing the Mission League in the playoffs for the City Championship."

The Jefferson Heights team ran out onto the field as the audience began cheering and applauding.

Kai wandered through the crowd, mingling with his teammates and fans, and receiving pats on his back from total strangers.

Coach Lindsey approached him and offered his hand. "Congratulations, Ryan. It seems like the team you play for always manages to win the tough one."

"Thank you, coach. Thank you for last year. I learned a lot from you."

"I got at least a dozen calls from college coaches this past week. Three or four of them asked about you."

"Who were they?"

"Just a couple of small little schools, one from Oregon, another from Arizona, another from some small town in Indiana. They're scouting for running backs."

"Indiana?"

"A school in a town called South Bend."

"South Bend? Notre Dame is in South Bend. What did you tell them?"

"I told them to make sure they had a scout here tonight."

Kai smiled. "Thank you, coach!"

A serious look crossed Lindsey's face. "I'm afraid we did not do a real good job of protecting you tonight. We should've figured out what Adams was up to and stopped him."

"All I wanna' do, coach, is to forget about what happened, and get on with life." Kai looked away, trying to conceal his emotions.

Lindsey put a hand on Kai's shoulder.

On another part of the field, Coach Ferrentini saw Joe Meyers intently watching him from the bleachers, cigar in mouth, smoke curling up around his puzzled face. Ferrentini slowly brought up his right hand, clutching a rolled-up play sheet, and showed Meyers his middle finger in a gesture of defiance.

Meyers nodded, just a hint of a smile.

Kai wandered amidst the celebrating crowd and found Buster Hollister approaching him with a goofy smile on his face. He tried to get away. Too late. Buster rushed forward and gave Kai a bear hug.

"Man, can you believe it, cornpone? I got a touchdown!"

Kai smiled. "How did it feel having a whole team chase your ass down the field, *Lucius*?"

"Awesome, Moore, awesome. I was scared to death, but God, it was awesome. Do you think they'd let me play fullback in college?"

Kai laughed.

Someone tapped Kai's shoulder and he turned to see who it was.

It was Denise.

He grabbed her and gave her a big hug. After a moment, he let her go. She drew back, a smile on her face while pretending to brush off the dirt off her blouse.

"Hangin' out with the enemy? What will your homies think?" Kai said.

"I don't care what they think. What have you got goin' on with that girl?"

"What girl? . . . Oh, Patty? . . . Nothing's goin' on! She's just a friend."

"Well, she flashed you."

"She's just a Drew Barrymore wannabe. Are you jealous?"

"Not me! But if I did what she did, they would've kicked me out of school and locked me up in Juvie Hall."

"You got a car now? How about meeting me for dogs and beer up in the Heights tonight?"

"Dogs and beer?"

"Well, hot dogs and root beer. You'd get to meet Patty. She serves up hotdogs and a running commentary on her brother's anatomy."

"Where do I meet you?"

On the field, the team, the band, and the cheerleaders were still noisily celebrating the victory. The band played their victory song and the cheerleaders, and the fans rocked to the music.

Kai scanned the audience. Some of the fans were waving at him and several people started shouting his name.

Suddenly, Kai felt as if he was no longer there. He was on a different field, wearing a different uniform, celebrating a different victory. He saw his mother standing in the bleachers as she did at the end of every game a year ago.

Nora Wilson made eye contact with her son. She smiled, a look of pride on her face.

Kai, now in a battered Saint Ignatius uniform, returned the smile and waved at her.

Nora Wilson waved back at her son.

Kai, now in Jefferson Heights uniform, tears in his eyes, had a smile on his face, as he walked off the field.

Author's Bio

The author, Ted Kozak, has officiated high school football for twenty-seven years in California and Kentucky and is a proud veteran of the United States Marine Corps. After retiring at the rank of Captain after twenty-six years of service with the Los Angeles Police Department, he worked for ten years as an attorney in California and another ten years in Kentucky. He lives in rural Kentucky with his wife and two dogs.

He is the author of *Charlie Wolf's Revenge, Charlie Wolf's Justice, The Messiah's Spy, Alex and Christina–Saving Lumenaria, Teresa–The Snake Witch, Lydia Harte, and Lydia Harte's Revenge.*

Printed in the U.S.